LIBRARIES

3 8003 21098 6978

KT-547-487

THE
BIGWOOF
CONSPIRACY

DASHE ROBERTS

STICKY PINES

WHERE THINGS
GET WEIRD

nosy
crow

For J & M

First published in the UK in 2020 by Nosy Crow Ltd
The Crow's Nest, 14 Baden Place,
Crosby Row, London SE1 1YW

Nosy Crow and associated logos are trademarks and/or registered
trademarks of Nosy Crow Ltd

Text © Dashe Roberts, 2020
Cover and chapter opener illustrations copyright © Bill Bragg, 2020

The right of Dashe Roberts to be identified as the author of this work
has been asserted.

All rights reserved

1 3 5 7 9 10 8 6 4 2

This book is sold subject to the condition that it shall not, by way of
trade or otherwise, be lent, hired out or otherwise circulated in any
form of binding or cover other than that in which it is published.
No part of this publication may be reproduced, stored in a retrieval
system, or transmitted in any form or by any means (electronic,
mechanical, photocopying, recording or otherwise) without the prior
written permission of Nosy Crow Ltd.

A CIP catalogue record for this book is available from the British Library

Printed and bound in Great Britain by Clays Ltd, Elcograf S.p.A.
Typeset by Tiger Media

Papers used by Nosy Crow are made from wood grown in
sustainable forests.

ISBN: 978 1 78800 686 6

www.nosycrow.com

CHAPTER 1

Encounter of a Weird Kind

After all the times she had insisted that something was out there, after all the times no one believed her, after the lifetime of sniggering she had endured – tonight, Lucy Sladan would prove she was right.

With a CLICK, she loaded a roll of film into the old camera she had "borrowed" from her parents. She needed proof, the kind that was hard to fake. *People of the world*, she thought, *prepare to learn the Truth*.

Her skin tingled with excitement. She still couldn't quite believe it. Just the night before, while taking the dog out for a gallop in the woods,

Lucy had seen something in the sky; something that looked remarkably, amazingly, like the out-of-focus flying objects pictured on her favourite website: *TheTruthHasLanded.org*.

A flash of lightning outside the round attic window cast jagged shadows across the sloped walls. For a fleeting moment, Lucy's bedroom seemed full of motion. She twisted a lock of purple hair and counted out six Mississippis before she heard the corresponding rumble of thunder. Pushing her plastic-framed glasses up the bridge of her nose, she reread a highlighted article in yesterday's newspaper:

SECOND DISAPPEARANCE
IN STICKY PINES

Beloved candy-store owner, Mandy Millepoids, 66, has been reported missing. He was last seen birdwatching in Molasses Grove on the evening of September 1. Meanwhile, police are still searching for factory worker Alastair Chelon, 37, last seen fishing at Black Hole Lake on August 17. Authorities are looking into sightings of large wild animals in the area.

Wild animals, Lucy scoffed. She knew the truth. *These guys weren't attacked. They were abducted. By ALIENS.*

She imagined the article they would write about her tomorrow: *Lucy Sladan, 12-year-old genius, rescues missing Sticky Pines residents while awesomely confirming once and for all the existence of extraterrestrials. Former critics are amazed and deeply apologetic.*

All she needed to do now was sneak out without getting caught.

A knock on the door sent the newspaper flying out of her hands in a dozen fluttering pieces. Her nine-year-old sister Willow entered without waiting for an invitation. Lucy wondered why she bothered to hang the "Keep Out, Unbelievers" sign on the door.

"What are you doing up here?" asked Willow. "Listening for radio signals from space?"

"Too much cloud cover." Lucy glanced at the clipping from *The ET Bee* pinned to the corkboard above her desk. The headline read:

"Do Aliens Use Bad Weather to Hide from Sight?" Lucy knew the answer: *You bet they flippin' do.* She gathered up the newspaper and put it back together in no particular order. "I think I'm gonna hit the hay early tonight."

"Your bedtime's not for two hours," said Willow.

"What can I say?" Lucy stretched her arms and yawned, fairly convincingly. "I'm bushed."

"You're not in your pyjamas."

"I was … just about to change." *Keep it together, Lucita. Sneaking out is all in the details.* She had googled it.

Willow kicked a pile of dirty clothes and hopped over to sit on the rumpled bed. "Did you hear there was another Bigfoot sighting?" She chewed the strings of her pink unicorn hoodie. "Dad says Sasquatches only eat boys, but Mom says they're equal opportunity."

Lucy snorted. "Please. Only babies and tourists believe in dumb stuff like Bigfoot."

"You believe in fairies," Willow sneered.

4

"I believe in transdimensional beings who've been MISTAKEN for fairies."

"Whatever." Willow rolled her eyes. "Errol ran off after dinner again. You're not supposed to feed him people food."

"Eating only dog food is boring, Will." Lucy checked the clock. "Did you want something?"

"Mom and Dad wanna know if you're gonna come make up songs with us," said Willow.

Three nights in a row? "Thanks for the invite, but like I said, I'm bushed."

"It's only eight o'clock," Willow complained. "What are you, five?" She picked up a toy Yoda from the bookshelf and started messing with its ears.

Lucy snatched the precious Jedi out of her hands. "OK, time to go."

"I wasn't gonna break your doll."

"Figurine," Lucy corrected. She scooted her sister out to the golden pine landing. "Tell Mom and Dad not to wake me up. It's a school night."

"Fine." Willow stuck out her tongue and,

mercifully, headed downstairs.

Lucy turned off all the lights and got into bed fully clothed. She stared impatiently into darkness until it was well past Willow's nine o'clock bedtime. Nobody came upstairs to check on her. *It's time.*

She slipped on her hiking boots, red hoodie and grey rain poncho, grabbed her backpack and tiptoed down the stairs, keeping her feet on the inside edges to minimise creaking. Cautiously, she inched her way along the hallway of the weathered log cabin. She ducked behind the kitchen island to avoid being seen by her parents in the living room, then slid out the side door and into the garage. The twangs of her father's banjo and her mother's cackling laughter faded as she dipped under the garage door – always open halfway so that Errol could get in and out.

Outside, a bolt of lightning splintered through the low clouds, the sky briefly resembling an undulating sea of jellyfish.

Lucy headed into the ancient moss-draped forest. She had grown up in these woods, and she and Willow had given names to the most distinctive-looking trees.

"Hey, Arnold." She saluted a knobby blue pine that had fallen sideways but managed to find a way to keep growing; its contorted two-pronged trunk twisting to resemble a capital letter A. She steered clear, knowing from experience that its bark was thick with dark, glue-like sap. A gust of wind allowed its tangled branches to shudder in response.

When the path came to a fork, she pulled out a hand-drawn map, oriented herself, then tramped off-road, straight into the shadowy foliage.

Twice, she slipped on the muddy ground and nearly lost her balance. She picked up a fallen tree branch, shook off a yellow banana slug as big as her forearm and snapped off the narrow end to make a walking stick.

Stabilised, she set off again, rain spattering her glasses. She wiped the lenses with her sleeve and scanned the patches of sky for any sign of unnatural activity. As she picked her way around a patch of brambles, she heard something out of place – a dull mechanical hum echoing above the forest. Lucy's heart began to pound. *This could be it.*

Squinting at the leafy shadows overhead, she ran towards whatever was making the artificial noise. It seemed to be hovering just over her head, hidden by the canopy. A glint of blue light darted across an opening in the leaves as the flying object she could not identify shot off deeper into the woods, the mosquito-like hum growing fainter by the second.

Oh no you don't! Lucy chased after it, twigs whipping at her cheeks. She leapt over an overgrown patch of ferns and slid on a slimy patch of mud, sprawling face-first on the soggy forest floor.

Out of breath, she rolled on to her back, the rain falling on her face. She was in a clearing in the trees under the stormy sky. There was no sign of the Unidentified Flying Object. *Come on, come on, I know you're out there.* She shivered. Her trousers were soaked through and she felt cold to the bone.

Then she heard an unmistakable sound: footsteps. Lucy hopped to her feet and clutched her walking stick. *Who would be crazy enough to be out here on a night like this? Besides me, I mean.*

CRUNCH. CRUNCH. CRUNCH.

Something was moving through the trees behind her. Something big. Anxiously, she remembered the news report about "large animals" in the area. Maybe the missing people really did get eaten by a mountain lion...

She brought the stick over her shoulder like a baseball bat and closed her eyes – then, "HIYAAHHH!" She spun at the darkness, swinging her staff blindly, hitting nothing. A burst of lightning revealed a large creature, wiry grey hair matted to its muscled frame, grimacing to reveal long, sharp teeth.

Lucy dropped the stick.

"Errol!" She had never been so happy to see the family wolfhound in her life. "Oh man, I'm sorry, bud!" She smiled with relief and took a step towards her shaggy pet. "C'mere, doggo."

But Errol wasn't looking at her, he was looking past her, and he clearly did not like what he was looking at.

Ears flat, he snarled in the kind of menacing display usually reserved for the weird guy who ran the candy store at the centre of town. *The guy who disappeared the other night.*

"What is it?" Lucy's smile faded. She wasn't sure whether she wanted to see what was frightening the forty-kilo dog, or if she should rethink her life choices and run home, not stopping until she was in bed with the dinosaur covers pulled over her head.

Curiosity won out over her sense of self-preservation. Slowly, she turned around.

What the...? For a moment, she forgot to breathe.

Not six metres away, cloaked in shadow near

the edge of the clearing, stood a massive hunch-backed figure staring up at the sky. It looked almost human, except for the stringy, tangled hair that hung wetly over its pot-bellied body, like some kind of golem made of moss.

From where Lucy was standing, it looked like those pictures in tourist traps throughout the valley. The ones they sold to suckers.

Holy. Flippin'. Crudballs. "Bigfoot?" she whispered.

The creature swivelled its head like a grotesque bird of prey, its massive body motionless. It issued a low, insect-like hiss from deep within its throat. A bolt of lightning flashed, revealing wide-set black eyes on a blunt, bulldoggish face.

That doesn't look like any Bigfoot picture I've ever seen… Her heart thundered in her chest. She was unable to move; out of awe or fear, she couldn't say.

Errol barked ferociously and lunged towards the hideous thing. The monster unhinged its froggish head and let out a dissonant wail, like a wolf being attacked by a swarm of bees.

Whoa.

Errol panicked and bolted through the trees, whimpering pitifully as he ran towards home.

"B-buddy?" Lucy swallowed. Errol was gone.

The monster tilted its head and stared at Lucy, its muscular, too-long arms hanging limply at its sides. She couldn't leave, not now. Not without proof of what she'd seen.

The bipedal beast swivelled its gaze back to the sky. Lucy strained to see what it was looking at, but saw nothing beyond the swirling gloom.

Then she heard it – the eerie electrical humming sound. Following the noise, she spotted something hovering high above the clearing: four ghostly blue lights set in a diamond formation.

Her skin prickled. This was it, the supernatural proof she had been searching for. *A real-life UFO and a freaky Bigfoot, both at the same time!* She could already picture the image on the cover of *Weird Enquiries Weekly.* This was by far the greatest day of her life.

Regaining the ability to reason, she dug the camera out of her backpack and unscrewed the lens cap with shaking hands. If she pulled this off, she would be a hero. They might even rename the town in her honour. *Welcome to Sladanville, where things get weird!*

She brought the camera to her eyes. *Crudberries.* She could see nothing but darkness. Hastily, she checked to make sure the camera's flash was on. She was going to need it.

The exquisitely weird creature whined like a walrus and pointed at the hovering lights, its crooked finger raised as if in awe.

Don't worry, Ugly, I see it too.

Lucy took a deep breath. She pointed the camera, hoping to get both the creature and the UFO in frame. *This is going to be epic…*

She fumbled for the trigger, and pressed. The flash went off. The creature screamed. There was a blinding bright light, a tremendous, deafening boom and then, darkness.

CHAPTER 2

Stranger Danger

Lucy came to, shivering and soaking wet. Her ears were ringing and her brain was throbbing. She groped at her surroundings, a vague impression of light and sound floating in and out of her hazy memory. *Did I finally get abducted by aliens?* Her fingers closed around a handful of mud and twigs. She was still in the forest. *How disappointing.*

With some effort, she forced her eyelids open, one by one. She found herself staring into a pair of angelic blue eyes surrounded by a hazy halo of yellow.

Oh cripes, am I dead?

"Thank goodness, you're alive!" said a far-off-sounding voice coming from the direction of the eyes.

That settles that question. Lucy grunted and tried to stand, but her legs wouldn't cooperate and she collapsed next to a purple-veined fern. She managed to get to her feet and felt pine needles stabbing through her waterlogged socks. For some reason, she was no longer wearing shoes.

"Are you OK?" said the blurry yellow being.

"Blarghgle," said Lucy.

"That doesn't sound very promising," said the voice. "I should probably call for help." The bell-shaped blob moved around her, a small glowing object in its hand trailing light in the darkness. "Ugh, there's never any reception in this town. How do you people survive?"

Lucy flinched as something pointy was shoved into her hand, then chirped with glee when she realised it was her glasses. She put them on and the world came into glorious focus. She was still in the clearing. Standing before her was a clean-cut boy about her age wearing a fancy yellow raincoat and galoshes. The matching rain hat was too big for his head, making it look about twice the normal size. He grinned as if she looked just as ridiculous to him as he did to her.

He extended his hand. "My name's Milo Fisher. What's yours?"

Fisher… Why does that name sound familiar? Lucy opened her mouth to speak but a wave of nausea hit. She bent over and retched the remains of her dad's meatloaf on the soggy forest floor. When she was done, her headache was gone and there was a warm hand rubbing gently between her shoulder blades.

"Do you need an ambulance?" asked Milo. "Are there even ambulances out here?"

Lucy laughed. "Yeah," she croaked. "There's ambulances out here. But let's not get one. I'm OK."

"I can't believe you survived that," he continued. "I've never seen anything like it, and

I've seen pretty much everything."

Survived what? The events of the evening came back to her in a series of hectic images. Lucy focused on two in particular. *The big hairy creature. The hovering lights.* She took a step and stumbled, latching on to Milo's outstretched arm.

"Camera," she said. "Where's my camera?"

"I think you should sit down," said Milo.

Lucy started digging through the leaves on the ground. "You don't understand. I need my camera, and I need it now."

Milo held his shiny platinum smartphone up high. "Still no reception," he sighed.

"Reception is for city folk," said Lucy.

"At least it's not raining any more. The storm stopped right after you got hit."

Lucy looked up at the night sky. It was true. The clouds had parted, the mossy forest was again alive with the sound of insects and amphibians. Above them, an endless sea of stars twinkled in a moonless sky. Below, the mud remained, and she was covered in it from head to toe.

"Camera, camera, camera," she repeated through chattering teeth. "Where is it? It can't have just vanished." She tripped over her hiking boots three metres from where she had regained consciousness. Milo, stronger than he looked, caught her around the waist.

"Sit down, will you?" he said. "You're in shock or something."

Lucy sat on a tree stump and rubbed her hands together to keep them from shaking.

Milo marched off, using his phone as a flashlight. He picked up something from the ground and unfolded it. "Did you draw this map yourself?"

"Yeah."

"Wow. It's really detailed. What do the red Xs mean?"

"They're potential sightings of ... uh, nothing. Can I have it, please?" asked Lucy.

"Of course." He handed it over, then located one of Lucy's boots. A slow trail of clear slime dripped down from the toe. "Ew," he grimaced.

Lucy wrinkled her nose. "I must've stepped on a banana slug."

Milo stuck out his tongue and resumed his search. "Um … is this what you meant by 'camera'?" he asked, holding out a rather soggy-looking Fuji point-and-click.

"Yes!" Lucy grabbed the precious device out of his hands. "Nooo," she moaned.

"What?" asked Milo.

"It's all wet," she whimpered. "My life is over."

"Just buy a new one like a normal person. I think they sell old ones like this at antique shops."

Lucy took a deep breath. "It's OK, it's OK," she repeated to herself. "Maybe the film inside isn't damaged." She flipped the camera over and her heart dropped into her stomach. The back panel was open, water dripping everywhere. The camera was toast. The picture was ruined. She dropped to her knees and punched the ground with all her might.

Milo tossed her backpack at her feet. "I think you might have brain damage. We need to get help. Can you walk or should I carry you?"

"Carry me?" Lucy looked at him sideways. They were practically the same size.

He nodded cheerfully.

She took note of his perfectly coordinated rain gear, none of which was appropriate for hiking in the woods. She had never seen him before, and people so smartly dressed hardly ever came to Sticky Pines. *What horse did this kid ride in on?*

Lucy sat back on the tree stump. "I'm OK," she said. "I just need to get home." She put on her boots, brushed herself off and stood up. She did a couple of jumping jacks. "See?"

Milo looked doubtful, and the jumping jacks made Lucy's headache come back.

"You know, you never actually told me your name," he said.

"Oh," she said. "Lucy Sladan."

Milo held out a hand. "You're supposed to shake it," he said, after a moment.

"Right." She put her hand in his and he shook it matter-of-factly. *Yeah. You're not from around here.*

"Well, Lucy Sladan," said Milo, "you look pretty good for someone who just got struck by lightning. Aside from all the mud and sticks and stuff."

She stared at him blankly. "Struck by what now?"

"You'd think you'd be on fire or something. Is your hair supposed to be that purple?"

"Did you say lightning?" Lucy dug around in her backpack for a pen and her notebook, which she opened to a relatively scribble-free page. "Start from the beginning," she said. "What *exactly* did you see? Also, where did you come from and what are you doing here?"

"Whoa. Wait a minute." Milo raised his palms. "I don't see a badge, officer. Why don't you start?"

"Me?" Lucy crumbled a clump of dirt that was caked to her eyebrows. "I live over there," she pointed over her shoulder, "and I'm out here because I was looking for…" She paused, pondering the events of the night and how improbable it all seemed. *He'll never believe me.*

"What's the matter?" asked Milo. "Is it a secret or something?"

Lucy scowled. "I hate secrets. If everybody knew the truth the world would be a better place."

"That's a bold statement."

She took a deep breath. "I was out here chasing a UFO, OK?" She paused for the inevitable laughter.

"A UFO?" said Milo.

"Unidentified Flying Object," said Lucy.

"I know what it means."

"I also saw a big hairy creature that might have been a Sasquatch."

"A sask-what?" asked Milo.

"The famous cryptozoological creature?" said Lucy.

"Crypto-zoo-a-huh?"

"Bigfoot."

"Oh, right. Wow," said Milo. "UFO. Bigfoot. That's … wow."

"You must have seen it. It was just over there." She ran to where the creature had stood moments ago, arms outstretched to indicate its enormous size. "And the UFO was right up there," she pointed.

Milo shook his head. "All I saw was a jagged flash of light and your flying body. I didn't see any Bigfoot." He smirked.

There it is. "You don't believe me."

"Well, I mean, come on," he chuckled.

How predictable. Nobody would ever believe her. Not without proof. Proof she still didn't have.

"Forget it," said Lucy. "Thanks for making sure I wasn't dead or whatever." She shoved her broken camera into her backpack and stomped off.

"Hey, wait a minute!" Milo chased after her.

"Sorry," she said, hopping over a fallen log. "I don't bring home strangers."

"I'm not a stranger." Milo jogged to catch up. "We're practically neighbours. And, feel free to laugh at me," he smiled, "but I was out here doing an art project."

Lucy hoisted her backpack higher on her shoulders. "An art project?" she asked. "In the storm?"

"I was trying to capture the nuances of the lightning."

Lucy skipped around a log and on to the path that led back to her house. "Where's your paintbrush?"

"I'm not that kind of artist," he said. "I was following the storm when I stumbled into your clearing. It's a shame I didn't get a picture of you being electrified. I could've won a Pulitzer." He hopped gingerly over a bullfrog. "I was taking pictures with a slow shutter speed, but they kept coming out all blurry. Then I figured out how to use the ISO—"

"Wait a minute." Lucy stopped. "You have a camera?"

"Indubitably." He pulled an expensive-looking digital camera out of his coat pocket.

"You have a camera." Lucy dropped her bag and stared at the boy as if seeing him for the first time.

"Like I said," said Milo, slowly this time, "I. Was. Taking. Pictures."

CHAPTER 3

Bigwoof

Lucy awoke to a bright light and a metallic clatter.

"Arise, young warrior, and face the day," said her father, securing the metal blinds at the sunny attic window. He was dressed for work at the Sticky Sweet factory. His dark-green coveralls had his name, "Silas", stitched over a juggling clown, the company mascot.

"Five more minutes," Lucy groaned, blocking the sunlight with her arm.

"I thought you went to bed early last night." Silas smoothed his black moustache in the full-length mirror.

"Indubitably," mumbled Lucy. She sat up and immediately flopped back down again. "I feel super rested."

Silas switched on the clock radio at the head of Lucy's bed. She flinched.

"The weather station?" he asked. "Seriously?" He tuned it to classic rock, turned the volume up high and bobbed his head to the harmonica solo in "Run Through the Jungle". "Eggs and toast are on the table, and you're leaving for school in thirty minutes." He left the room playing air guitar.

Lucy stared up at a poster of an astronaut floating in space and replayed the previous night in her head. *What were those lights in the sky? Was I really struck by lightning? What was that strange creature?* And most baffling of all: *What is the deal with Milo Fisher?*

He had walked her home, using his phone as a compass and talking all the while. His family had moved to Sticky Pines about two months ago. He was in eighth grade, one year above her, and he was somehow aware that they had the same lunch period. He'd taken a lot of convincing to agree to let her see his photos.

"They're not ready to share," he had insisted. "I need to edit them first, crop them, bring out the colour."

"Don't do that," Lucy pleaded. "I'm sure they're perfect. You seem like a genius. You practically saved my life, right?"

"I guess you could say that," he said with a winning smile.

She pulled the sleeve of his rain slicker. "Promise me you won't edit them. The pictures have to show nothing but the absolute truth."

"Well…" He bit his lip. "OK. I'll show them to you, unedited, if you agree to come over for dinner first. I only show my work to friends. Do we have a deal?"

Milo held out his hand. Lucy shook it.

An overwhelmingly enthusiastic Errol greeted them when they reached the Sladan family's cabin on Foxglove Lane.

The dog gave Milo a cursory sniff, then tackled Lucy and licked most of the mud off her face. She was annoyed that he had deserted her, but she couldn't really blame him. Not everyone had the stomach to confront the very boundaries of this plane of existence.

"Well," said Milo, scratching the dog behind the ears, "I'd better get back before they notice I'm not on the premises." He waved goodbye and disappeared back into the forest, the light from his phone leading the way.

It occurred to Lucy that it was probably *she* who ought to have been walking *him* home through the woods that night. When she finally peeled off her muddy clothes and flopped into bed, it was well past midnight.

The school day dragged on. Each class seemed longer than the last. Lucy pinched herself to stay awake in English. As usual, she had been one of the only students to actually do the summer reading, and poor Mrs Stricks had to spend the whole class summarising.

While the tie-dye-clad teacher was busy drawing a giant squid on the blackboard, Lucy passed an intricately folded note to her best friend, Tex, who was doodling at his desk three rows over.

"X-ed the frontier once again," Lucy had written, *"and I've got PROOF. Deets @ lunch."*

Tex gave Lucy a thumbs-up.

"Mr Arkhipov." Mrs Stricks pointedly cleared her throat. "Miss Sladan."

Tex quickly went back to drawing a dragon on his binder and Lucy returned to pinching herself to stay awake.

At last, the lunch bell rang. Lucy stuffed her books into her still-damp backpack as quickly as she could.

"Lucita?" said Mrs Stricks. "A moment, please?"

"Uh-oh," Tex whispered as he passed Lucy's desk. "You are in trouble with the brain police." He clapped her on the back. "Be strong."

Lucy pounded her chest with a fist.

Tex paused in the doorway. "I will catch you in the cafeteria," he said. "I cannot wait to hear your latest story."

"It's gonna change your life!" she called after him.

Mrs Stricks cleared a space between the stacks of paper on her desk and laid out her lunch. This included pesto pasta, an apple, three chocolate chip cookies and a can of Nu Co. Cola.

"It's the second week of school and you're already passing notes in class," she said, going for a cookie first. "Would you like one?" she offered as she took a bite. "The missus baked them from scratch."

Something Lucy appreciated about living in a small town was that everyone knew everything about everybody else. Mrs Stricks's wife was known as "the Other Mrs Stricks" and she was a bit of an odd duck. Some folks said she was crazy, some even said she was a witch, but everybody agreed she was far and away the best baker in town.

"Ooh, yes, please," said Lucy. She accepted a cookie and took an eager bite.

"Now, my dear," said Mrs Stricks, flicking a stray crumb off her desk, "which medieval torture method do you think your mother would employ if she caught you passing notes in *her* class?"

Lucy's mother was the school science teacher, a fact that meant it was nearly impossible for Lucy to get away with anything other than scholastic perfection. "I'm super sorry, Mrs Stricks. I swear I won't pass notes again. Please don't tell my mom."

Mrs Stricks contemplated her cookie. "I'm concerned you're letting yourself get distracted again, my dear. We don't want a repeat of last year, do we? Falling asleep in class, forgetting to turn in assignments…"

"No, ma'am," Lucy nodded solemnly.

"Try to stay focused on what's really important this year, hmm?"

"I will. I promise." Lucy waved politely and hurried out the door.

What's more important, she thought as she ran down the hallway, *lectures on books, or discovering things for people to write books about?* She was pretty sure she had her priorities in order.

She hustled over to the cafeteria, which perpetually smelled like every kind of food at once.

Sliding her lunch tray along the railing, Lucy stood on tiptoe to see if she could spot Milo Fisher in the crowd. No luck. Hopefully he had made it home OK, what with monsters lurking in the woods and all. She was surprised she hadn't noticed him before, seeing how ... noticeable he was.

The cafeteria lady handed her a plate of fried food and a carton of chocolate milk, and Lucy made her way to the back tables to sit with Tex.

Alexei "Tex" Arkhipov had been her best friend since first grade, when his family moved to Sticky Pines from "the mothership", which is what Lucy called Russia. They had eaten lunch at the same table since they hit the upper grades.

Tex greeted her with a nod. "So what happened? Did you finally get abducted?"

"I wish," she sighed.

"Did you get a boyfriend or something?"

"What? No." Her cheeks reddened. "This is way bigger than that."

"Big like the chupacabra living under your porch?"

"That thing was way too nasty to be a badger."

"Big like the poltergeist haunting Hank's Super Saver?"

"It's unusually cold in the frozen food section."

"Big like the sea monster in Black Hole Lake?" Tex splurted the contents of a fifth ketchup packet on his plate.

Lucy scowled. She'd never live that one down. Tex's mother still wouldn't let them go out on the lake without supervision. But seriously, that log strongly resembled an abyssal sea serpent. Anyone with the tiniest bit of knowledge on the subject would have made the same mistake.

"You really need to learn how to swim," she grumbled.

"Not in Black Hole Lake I do not." He crunched a ketchup-coated fish stick.

"Anyway," Lucy grinned smugly, "it doesn't matter." She had spotted Milo across the room, cleaner and wearing far less plaid than anyone in a ten-mile radius. "My proof is here."

Milo waved as he pardoned his way past a table of curious athletes and cheerleaders. "You clean up nicely," he said when he arrived.

"Thanks," said Lucy. "I showered."

Tex dropped his fish stick, splattering ketchup on to the faux-granite tabletop. Milo tapped his foot and looked around absently. After nobody said anything for a moment, Lucy realised she was supposed to introduce them.

"Oh. Milo, this is Tex Arkhipov," she gestured. "Tex, this is Milo Fisher."

Milo reached out a hand for him to shake. Tex slapped it.

"Fisher…" Tex snapped his fingers. "Your father just bought the Sticky Sweet Company, did he not?"

"Indeed he did," said Milo.

Lucy slapped her forehead. "That's why I know the name. My dad works at Sticky Sweet."

"Small world," said Milo. He sat next to Lucy and unfolded a slick black lunchbox that was clearly from the future. He opened a small glass container of bright-green beans and started eating them with a metal spork.

"Is that edamame?" asked Tex.

"You want some?" asked Milo.

"*Arigato.*" Tex bowed.

Amused, Milo passed Tex the container. "How's your headache?" he asked Lucy. "Have you recovered from last night?"

"You were there too?" Tex looked at Lucy incredulously. "What the plop have you been up to, Lucille? And on a Tuesday, no less." He pounded the table. "Details, please."

"Well, firstly," said Milo, "Lucy got struck by lightning."

"Struck by what now?" Tex asked.

"That's *his* interpretation of events," said Lucy.

"Awesome," said Tex. "Did you get any superpowers?"

"X-ray vision," Lucy joked. "Nice Minion undies."

Tex sneered.

"Secondly," said Milo, pouring thick brown sauce over grilled chicken and white rice, "she says she saw mysterious blue lights in the sky."

"Pshhh," Tex scoffed. "I've heard that before."

"These were different," Lucy insisted.

"Did you get a picture?" asked Tex.

Lucy crossed her arms unhappily.

Tex chortled.

"And thirdly," said Milo, as if he were setting up the punchline to a joke, "she saw Bigfoot."

"Bigfoot?" Tex asked loudly. "Bigfoot, Lucille? This is your big news?"

Lucy's cheeks flushed as she heard laughter coming from the table behind her. "It's Lucita, beet eater," she huffed.

Tex pointed at her with a fish stick. "You have crossed a sacred line. You swore you would never stoop to squatcher level."

"Squatcher?" asked Milo.

"People obsessed with Sasquatch," Lucy muttered.

Milo chuckled while he chewed.

"I'm not even sure it was Bigfoot," said Lucy. "It looked ... weirder. It had the face of a bulldog."

"Like an ugly werewolf?" asked Milo, covering his mouth with his hand.

"So you saw 'Bigwoof'?" Tex laughed so hard he almost fell out of his chair.

Lucy threw a fry at Tex's head as Milo cracked up.

"None of you will be laughing after tonight," Lucy snipped.

Tex wiped a tear from his eye. "Why? What is

happening tonight?"

"Lucy is joining me for dinner," Milo answered.

"Is she?" said Tex, looking far too interested.

"After which we'll look through my photos for Evidence of the Unknown." Milo waved his fingers spookily.

Tex clucked his tongue as Lucy scraped up the last remains of ketchup with a soggy fry. "Where did you manage to find someone as loony as you on such short notice?" he asked.

"The woods." She shoved the fry in her mouth.

"Hey, Tex," a voice shouted from across the room. It was Toli, Tex's younger brother. "They are letting us play Zork in the library today. Show me how to beat the vampire bat?"

"Ooh. Classic game," said Tex. "Give me one minute!" He pushed out his chair and stood. "All right, you tinfoil hats, I am off. Anybody want to join me?"

"No thanks." Lucy waved. "Try not to get eaten by a grue."

"Solid advice," said Tex.

He saluted and marched off with his tray.

"He seems fun," said Milo. He took a sip of something green and healthy-looking from a plastic thermos.

"That's one way of putting it," said Lucy. She scooted her chair a bit closer. "So," she said, her voice low, "did you look through the pictures yet?"

Milo shook his head. "I was too tired last night. Anyway, I thought it'd be more exciting to wait."

"Exciting is an understatement," Lucy assured him. "Trust me, Milo Fisher. This is gonna blow your mind."

"That's a big claim, Lucy Sladan." He raised an eyebrow. "You wouldn't lie to me, would you?"

"Never," she said. "Think you can handle it?"

He grinned. "I guess we'll find out."

CHAPTER 4

Number 249

Following Milo's detailed instructions, Lucy turned off Douglas Road and cruised through an open gateway on to a long private driveway. The sparkly quartz gravel made a satisfying crunch under the tyres of her mountain bike. The Fishers' vast property was surrounded by a tall fence, making it one of the few places in Sticky Pines Lucy had never explored before.

The trees parted, revealing a tall modern lodge with glass walls all along the ground floor, quite distinct from the small pine cabins that customarily dotted the local landscape. *Jeez, do the Fishers live in a hotel?*

Lucy slid to a stop by the porch and set her bike on its kickstand. Catching her reflection in the window of a black SUV parked out front, she ran her fingers through her wind-mussed hair, then tromped up the steps and rang the bell. Milo appeared before the chimes stopped, his brown hair damp and freshly combed.

"You look spiffy," said Lucy.

"Can I take your coat?" Milo pointed to her orange fishing vest.

"No thanks, I'm good." She slipped her hands into her pockets. "So where are the pictures?"

"Come on, Lucy," Milo chided. "At least *pretend* that you came here simply for the pleasure of my company."

"Sorry." She forced a smile. "Business later. Dinner first."

They entered to the sound of Spanish guitar music. The whole house smelled like the beach at low tide. The high living-room ceiling was crisscrossed with smooth white beams. Towering windows overlooked a manicured yard surrounded by dense forest, at the edge of which a couple of deer delicately grazed. In the centre of the room sat a translucent glass cube with a fire blazing inside. There was no chimney that Lucy could see.

A thin woman wearing athletic gear and pearls greeted them as they entered. Her hair was long and smooth, bleached so blonde it was almost silver.

"Hello," she chirped. "You must be little miss Lucy."

"Nice to meet you, Mrs Fisher," Lucy replied.

"Oh, call me Kaitlyn." She stuck out a hand.

So many handshakes… Lucy wiped her hand on her jeans and shook. Up close the woman looked older than expected, though her skin was tight and smooth.

"Thank you for having me over," said Lucy.

"Oh, not at all," said Kaitlyn. "You sprouts look hungry. How about some snacks?" She slipped off to the kitchen, soon returning with a silver platter of appetisers on toothpicks.

Lucy picked up a purple and grey cube and popped it in her mouth. It was squishy and tasted like garlic. She forced herself to swallow, and hoped at least one of the other things was food she could actually eat.

"I just love your purple hair," said Kaitlyn, reaching out two fingers to feel Lucy's violet tresses. "Very bohemian."

"Thanks," said Lucy. She smoothed her hair behind her ears and wondered if she should dye it green again so people would stop touching it. "I like your hair dye too."

"Oh, aren't you sweet," said Kaitlyn. She wrinkled her nose. "I'll leave you two to chat while I check on the oyster soufflé."

Oysters. So that's what the smell is…

"Yum," said Milo, leading Lucy to a pair of white-leather armchairs facing the fire cube. "Do you like oysters?"

"I've never actually eaten one," said Lucy. "My dad calls them 'sea snot'."

Milo burst out laughing. "Don't mention that

to Kaitlyn," he warned. "She takes her seafood very seriously."

"You call your mom Kaitlyn?" said Lucy. She held out her hands and felt the warmth of the techno-magical fire.

"She's not my mom," said Milo. "She's my latest stepmom. She's been married to my dad almost three years now. It's practically a record."

"Where's your real mom?" asked Lucy.

"She died when I was six," said Milo. He picked at a blue fuzzball on his sweater. "She had cancer."

"Oh man, that's awful," said Lucy, horrified. "I'm so sorry."

"Thanks." He smiled tightly. "I've got my dad. He travels a lot but he takes me wherever he goes."

"That must be nice," said Lucy.

They stared into the fire cube. Lucy wondered if the logs were real, and if not, where the crackling sound was coming from.

"My dad should be back from the factory any

minute," said Milo. "He's sprucing up the whole business. You'll see, pretty soon people all over the country will be eating Sticky Sweet."

"That would be cool," said Lucy. "Outsiders don't usually like the piney taste. Is your dad changing the mascot? Clowns are creepy."

"No way," said Milo. "My dad loves clowns."

"Great." Lucy rolled her eyes. She picked up a cracker topped with orange paste from the appetiser tray and touched it to the tip of her tongue. It tasted like carrot. *I can do vegetables.* She scarfed it down and picked up two more.

A door slammed in another room and Milo perked up.

"Something sure smells good in here," said a deep, razor-sharp voice.

A tall man with a square chin and greying hair strode into the living room. Kaitlyn kissed him on the cheek and slid his suit jacket off his broad shoulders. She draped it elegantly over her arm, then took his briefcase and disappeared down the hallway.

Mr Fisher loosened his tie and ruffled his son's hair like in one of those black-and-white TV shows from the fifties.

"Hey there, kiddo," he said. He lifted Milo off the chair in a bear hug, then set him down and reached out a hand to Lucy, who was at this point quite prepared to shake it. "You must be Milo's new friend."

"Nice to meet you," she said. "This is a really sweet house."

"Good eye," he winked. "One of those Internet kids built it around the turn of the millennium." He took out his smartphone, platinum like Milo's, and pressed a few buttons. The music changed to 1940s croon and a glowing shelf filled with crystal bottles folded down from a smooth white wall. Mr Fisher walked over and clinked a large ice cube into a glass, then poured himself something yellowish.

"Interesting hair," he said to Lucy. "Very bold."

"Thanks," she said. For some reason she felt

the need to sit up straighter.

"Lucy's dad works at the factory," said Milo. "Do you know him?"

"What's his name?" asked Mr Fisher.

"Silas Sladan," said Lucy.

Mr Fisher shook his head. "He must work on the floor." He took a sip of his drink, the ice tinkling gently in his glass.

"My dad said you changed the name of the company," said Lucy. The Sticky Sweet Sticky Pines Sweetener Company employed many of the residents in the Big Crater Valley. It had been around for over a hundred years. "You're calling it Nu Co., right?"

"The Sticky Sweet Sticky Pines Sweetener Company only sells sweetener," said Mr Fisher. "We plan to get a little more creative with it. We're also changing the name of the sweetener to Nucralose."

"Nucralose," said Lucy. "That sounds kinda like the name of the sugar molecule: sucrose."

Mr Fisher's eyes twinkled. "You know your science."

"I told you she was smart," said Milo.

"My mom's a science teacher," said Lucy.

"How delightful." Mr Fisher raised his glass.

"Dinner's ready," Kaitlyn sang from another room.

They migrated to a dimly lit room with a magnificent view of the Big Crater Mountains. The music followed uninterrupted, emanating from unseen speakers as they took their seats around the table.

The food was unlike anything Lucy had ever encountered. She could identify nothing but bread rolls and a bowl of rice, which, on closer inspection, might not actually be rice. She scooped some on to her plate and hoped it tasted as bland as it smelled.

"So what are you crazy kids up to this evening?" asked Mr Fisher.

"I'm gonna show Lucy my art project," said Milo.

"Pardon me?" said his father.

"Going to," Milo corrected himself.

"What are you working on now?" asked Kaitlyn. "Abstract sculpture?"

"I thought he was doing stand-up comedy," said Mr Fisher. "Didn't we just buy him a ukulele?"

"Photography," Milo informed the table.

"That's my boy," chuckled Mr Fisher. "Always broadening his horizons. Smart as a whip. Tests extraordinarily well." His steely-blue eyes turned to Lucy. "Are you also a photographer?"

She felt like he was trying to see inside her head.

"She thinks I might have caught a picture of Bigfoot," Milo answered for her.

Lucy kicked him under the table.

"Bigfoot, eh?" Mr Fisher chuckled. "I haven't heard of a good old-fashioned Bigfoot sighting in a long time. Good for you. Curiosity didn't kill the cat, it was boredom."

"I totally agree," said Lucy, feeling more comfortable. *These people know what's up.*

"My my, you eat like a bird!" sang Kaitlyn. She heaped something lumpy and grey over Lucy's not-rice.

"But the creature she described sounds way weirder than Bigfoot," said Milo. "We're calling it Bigwoof."

"We're doing that officially now?" said Lucy.

Mr Fisher raised an eyebrow. "Bigwoof?" he asked. "You must have a wild imagination."

"Not really, sir," Lucy responded. "It's real. I saw it with my own eyes. It had the craziest howl…"

"You know," Milo mused, "I actually *could* have a picture of it on my camera, assuming it exists. I was using this wide-angle lens—"

"And where did you see all this, exactly?" Mr Fisher interrupted.

"Oh, it was past the creek out that way," Milo pointed. "Halfway between our house and Lucy's."

"Interesting," said Mr Fisher. He checked his phone. "Oh dear. It seems I missed a call."

"Wow, you get reception here?" asked Lucy.

"I get reception everywhere." Mr Fisher stood and kissed his wife on the cheek. "Apologies, darling. The food was delicious, as always." He paused on his way out and placed a heavy hand on Lucy's shoulder. "What did it look like?"

"Bigwoof?" Lucy asked, still chewing a rubbery oyster. She glanced at Milo, who nodded in encouragement. She swallowed. "It was amazing. Tall and hairy and weird, like a gorilla-bulldog-amphibian-hybrid thingy."

Mr Fisher stared thoughtfully out the window. "Bigwoof," he mused. "What will you kids think of next?"

Milo's second-floor bedroom was spacious and sparse. The bed was neatly made, the pale-blue walls decorated solely with a photo of Milo and his father on a sunny beach. A red-and-white striped chaise longue sat below an arched window. The only clutter occurred on the desk, which was littered with coloured pencils, electronic gewgaws and some black-and-white photos of pigeons and skyscrapers. A thin laptop sat at the centre, hooked up to a larger monitor.

Lucy whistled. "Nice big room you got here, Fish."

"Thanks," he said. "Fish? Is that a nickname?"

"It's shorter than Fisher," Lucy shrugged. "Plus, it's what your house smells like. No offence."

He nodded in approval. "I've never had a nickname before." He unravelled a cable and plugged the camera into the computer. "So how many pictures do you want to see? There are over four hundred."

"These could be the most important photographs in the history of mankind," said Lucy. "What do *you* think?"

Milo laughed. "I guess we'll be here for a while. Feel free to make yourself comfortable."

She kicked off her boots and sat cross-legged

in a swivel chair, spinning around once for good measure.

Milo enlarged the first image: a close-up of a green-and-yellow-streaked banana slug.

"Hey, that's not bad," said Lucy. "You really caught something in its eyes."

"Thanks," he smiled, clicking over to a pair of squirrels eating peanuts. "See anything interesting?" He zoomed in on the background and started scrolling around.

"Nothing yet."

"Two down," said Milo, "four hundred and twenty-three to go."

Around photograph two hundred and thirty-eight Lucy's eyes started to cross. She took off her glasses and rubbed her eyes.

"Don't tell me you're tired already," said Milo. He seemed like someone who could stay up for days and remain as chipper as a chipmunk. "Let's take a break. Do you like hot chocolate?"

"Hot chocolate as in regular hot chocolate?" asked Lucy.

"Yep," said Milo.

"Who doesn't?" said Lucy. "But I'm not taking a break."

"OK, Inspector Sladan. You keep going, I'll be back in a flash." He ran downstairs.

Lucy stifled a yawn and looked at her watch. It was already seven thirty. Her parents had made her promise she'd be home at eight o'clock on the dot. There was no way they were getting through all the photos that night. She slipped on her glasses and clicked through some more pictures. She stopped at number two forty-nine.

At first she mistook it for a shadow behind a moss-covered boulder. But then she noticed a familiar shape among the trees. She zoomed in and her stomach did a backflip. There it was. Clear as day and dark as night. A lanky, hairy, horrible, half-humanoid creature, standing among the trees and staring up at the sky. Lucy could almost hear its eerie wail.

She clasped her hand over her mouth and jumped out of her chair in amazement. "No.

Flippin'. Way." *Finally!*

She heard someone enter the room behind her. "Fish, you won't believe what I found!"

"Something intriguing, I presume?"

Lucy whipped around. Mr Fisher stood in the doorway, sipping a mug of hot cocoa.

"M-Mr Fisher," she stammered.

"What do we have here?" he asked. He set his mug by the computer and inspected the photograph.

"It's Bigwoof," Lucy uttered uncontrollably. "It's a real-life monster, right there in the flesh! Can you believe it?"

"Hmm." He leaned closer to the screen. "Well, would you look at that?" he said. "It seems my boy caught a picture of a bear. Milo's a fine photographer, isn't he?"

"Wait, what?" asked Lucy, looking back at the picture, confused. "That is *definitely* not a bear."

"Looks like one to me," he responded. With a quick flick of his wrist, his cup toppled over, depositing its frothy chocolate contents all over the computer and camera.

Lucy could only look on in horror.

"Oh dear." Mr Fisher shook his head. "Look at this mess. I'll have to clean it up before the electronics are destroyed. Not to worry." He unplugged the laptop and the precious photo disappeared from the monitor. He swept up the camera too, and headed for the door. "I've got everything under control."

Without another word, he disappeared down the stairs, leaving Lucy standing alone in shocked silence.

A furious anger bubbled under her skin. She tried to piece together what had just happened and how it had happened so quickly. *What the— Why? Why would he do that?* It took every ounce of self-control to keep from screaming.

Milo cleared his throat from the hallway. "Um. Lucy?" He entered the room sheepishly, carrying a tray of cheese and crackers and a couple of steaming mugs. "I just saw my dad…" He looked so nervous she almost felt sorry for him. "He said it was an accident. He's really sorry," he faltered.

Lucy stared at the ceiling to keep her tears from spilling on to her cheeks. "I had it," she said through gritted teeth.

"Had what?"

"The picture. Number two forty-nine. It was right there. And now it's gone."

"You saw a picture of Bigwoof?" asked Milo.

Lucy nodded.

"Are you sure it wasn't a bear? My dad said—"

"It wasn't a BEAR."

Milo stepped backwards, sloshing hot chocolate on to the tray.

Lucy counted to ten so she wouldn't throw her boot at the darkened computer monitor. "Sorry," she said. "It's just... Your dad spilled his drink on purpose. I saw him."

Milo frowned and set the tray on the desk. "He wouldn't do that."

"The picture was *right there*." She stared longingly at the darkened screen. "I *had* it."

Milo's expression was a mix of pity and confusion. "Look, Lucy, I'm sure there's a perfectly logical explanation for what you think you saw. I mean, it would be amazing if monsters were actually real, but at the end of the day, the world's a pretty predictable place."

"Monsters don't have to be supernatural, Fish. There's all kinds of weird things out there."

"Fair enough," he smiled. "We'll get the camera back soon, and if Bigwoof's there, we'll find him. I promise."

"If you say so," she mumbled. She checked her watch. "Crud. I have to go."

"But you didn't have any cheese and crackers." Milo pointed to the tray.

"Well, I am pretty hungry." Lucy grabbed a hunk of something crumbly, put it on a cracker and took a bite, then immediately spat it out on to the floor. "I thought you said this was cheese," she gagged, spewing crumbs everywhere.

"Yeah," Milo sighed, "that was the Point Reyes Blue."

Lucy skidded to a stop on her dirt driveway, out of breath, at eight minutes past eight. She was pretty sure she could talk her way out of being less than ten minutes late without getting into too much trouble. Sometimes she wished her parents cared about her just a tiny bit less.

She burst through the front door at full speed. "Sorry I'm late, I—"

Her mom paced anxiously behind the island in the kitchen. Her dad sat on a stool, the landline to his ear. They both looked extremely serious.

Uh-oh.

"Hey, sweetie," said her mother. She gave Lucy a tight squeeze. "Go join your sister, OK? We're on the phone with the sheriff. I'll explain everything later."

The sheriff? How much trouble am I in? Lucy's heart sank. *Could this day get any worse?*

She slumped into the living room. Willow was on the floor next to the wood-burning stove, working on a jigsaw puzzle of a great white shark.

"What's going on?" Lucy asked.

"You know Mrs Stricks?"

"The teacher or her wife?"

"Teacher," said Willow.

"What about her?"

"She's gone."

"What do you mean 'gone'? I just saw her today. She gave me a cookie."

"Her wife called and said that Mrs Stricks never came home after school." Willow looked up at her big sister, worried. "Do you think she disappeared? Like the others?"

"I ... I dunno, Will."

Lucy felt like she was sinking in quicksand. *What is going on?* It couldn't all be a coincidence. The disappearances. The lights in the sky. The monster in the woods. It all seemed connected. *But how?*

Something strange was happening in the town of Sticky Pines, and the only thing Lucy knew for certain was that no one could see it but her.

CHAPTER 5

The Other Mrs Stricks

For the first time in her life, Lucy skipped school. She knew her parents would destroy her if they found out, but there were more pressing things on her mind than social studies could address. And besides, hadn't she promised Mrs Stricks she would focus on what was truly important?

Before the first bell, she took a right instead of a left at Bessy the barn-red bell tower and headed out across the playground. With some effort, she hoisted her heavy backpack over the chain-link fence and hopped over into the woods.

Her parents' camera was still broken, so Lucy had filled her bag with plaster kits and bottled water in case she ran into any footprints of unusual size. By mixing plaster with water and pouring it into a footprint, it was possible to create a likeness of a creature's foot. It was a technique popular with squatchers and Girl Scouts.

What have I become? Lucy lamented as she slipped the dusty bag over her shoulders and hurried into the trees.

Lucy's parents had taken the day off to join a sizable search party for Mrs Stricks. Most of the teachers at school had done the same. As a result, Principal Pakuna had arranged a wilderness safety assembly that would take up most of the day. Lucy had it on good authority that puppets would be involved. She was sure she wouldn't be missed.

The search party was out looking for Mrs Stricks on the birding trail. Lucy was going to visit the Other Mrs Stricks.

Even if she's as crazy as people say, she has to know something.

Lucy zipped up her red hoodie and inhaled the crisp fall air. The leafy branches, slimy orange fungi and chittering wildlife usually set her mind at ease, but after the events of the last few weeks, the woods were starting to give her the heebie-jeebies. Twice, she thought she heard footsteps behind her, but when she turned she saw nothing but the wind through the ferns.

She picked up the pace, following a dirt road through a sparsely populated neighbourhood. Soon, she reached the Strickses' hand-built cottage nestled among a lofty grove of Douglas firs. A weathered wooden staircase connected the driveway to the raised porch. Elaborate carvings of owls, one at rest, one about to take flight, sat atop each bannister like watchful guardians.

"The owls are not what they seem," said a gravelly voice.

Lucy jumped before she realised that a tall woman with wild silver hair was speaking from the shadows behind the screen door.

"They're not barn owls, they're barred owls,"

the woman continued. A pair of round yellow sunglasses was perched at the end of her long nose. "The stripes have faded over time. Mrs Stricks will have to repaint them when she returns."

"You think she'll be back soon?" asked Lucy, hopeful.

"Of course she will," the woman snapped. "Twyla is as resourceful as they come, and quite formidable when the need arises. She'll be back before you can spit."

"I'm sure you're right," said Lucy, who was far from sure.

"I've been ordered to wait here in case she returns or phones home." The Other Mrs Stricks examined Lucy more closely. "You're one of the Sladan girls, aren't you? The funny one."

Funny? "Uh, yeah. May I come in? I won't take much of your time."

The Other Mrs Stricks pulled her shawl tighter around her shoulders and sniffed the air. "You might as well," she sighed. "I'm not about to start turning away children on a day like this."

Lucy fought the urge to inform her that she was practically a teenager and ran up the stairs two by two.

She was greeted by a strong earthy scent, like boiled mushrooms, as she entered the cosy cottage. The pine walls were lined with shelves filled with knick-knacks and talismans from tourist traps all across the state. Four different clocks ticked away in the spaces the shelves did not cover, each reading a different time. Lucy found the atmosphere oddly comforting, both strange and familiar at the same time.

The Other Mrs Stricks sat in an overstuffed floral armchair, slouching into her hand-knit pink-and-grey striped shawl. The glass coffee table was cluttered with used mugs, the dried-up teabag tags draped over their sides like wilted flowers.

"Would you like some tea?" she asked Lucy, who was busy shaking a snow globe from the Giant Shoe Museum of Seattle.

"Sure," said Lucy.

"Kettle's in the kitchen."

Lucy deposited her backpack in the living room and went through a pair of swinging barn doors into the rather whimsical kitchen.

The ceiling was painted a deep blue scattered with yellow stars, a globular white light at the centre resembling a full moon. Portraits of deer, raccoons, turtles and other wildlife dotted the walls. Above the sink hung a watercolour of two smiling owls on a gnarled tree branch. Lucy guessed they had all been painted by her teacher.

On the stove sat a large, steaming copper pot – clearly the source of the earthy smell. Inside, something brown and foamy was bubbling away. *Blergh*. Whatever the Other Mrs Stricks was making for dinner looked rather unappetising.

A box of mint tea and a freshly sliced lemon sat next to a kettle. Lucy flicked it on and grabbed a Paul Bunyan mug from the cabinet.

She located a jar filled with packets of the

new-and-improved sweetener, the word "Nucralose" printed in bold red letters. Ripping open two packets, she tore the creepy clown logo's head in half and dumped their contents into her tea.

Careful not to spill, Lucy returned to the living room and sat on a paisley love seat facing the armchair. She took a sip from her mug and nearly choked. *Yikes, this stuff's sweeter than it used to be.*

"So what do you want, Sladan?" The Other Mrs Stricks added a packet of sweetener to her own tea.

"Oh, um." Lucy tried to think of a good opening question while she rummaged through her backpack for her notebook. "Have you lived here long?"

"Mmm." The older woman nodded. "We land where we land, we make what we need."

Lucy smiled, though she wasn't quite sure what she meant.

"Correct me if I'm wrong, child," said the

Other Mrs Stricks, "but shouldn't you be in school?"

"I want to help Mrs Stricks, if I can." Lucy opened her notebook. "I have a couple of questions, if you don't mind."

"Questions, questions, all anybody has is questions," grumbled the Other Mrs Stricks. She eyed Lucy's notebook. "What kind of answers have you got in there?"

"That's what I'm working on," said Lucy.

The Other Mrs Stricks grunted and adjusted her shawl.

Lucy checked her list of questions. "Can you think of any connection between Mrs Stricks and the people who disappeared? Mr Millepoids and Mr Chelon?"

"All things are connected," said the Other Mrs Stricks. "People are never really alone, you know. Any given person's really about a dozen mixed together."

"So that's a … yes..." Lucy's brow furrowed. *This might be harder than I thought.* She moved on to the next question on her list. "Did either of you see anything strange in the woods recently?"

"Strange?" The Other Mrs Stricks adjusted the chain on the cuckoo clock by her chair. "What do you mean, strange? Top hats and toe socks are strange."

"Have you noticed any large creatures around?"

"There are often black bears about."

"I'm not talking about bears," said Lucy. She flipped through the pages of her notebook and held up a rudimentary picture she had drawn of Bigwoof. "I mean something big and weird and hairy that walks on two legs."

The Other Mrs Stricks blinked coldly. "Please, child, tell me you aren't talking about Bigfoot at a time like this."

"Well, I—"

"What are you, Sladan?" The old woman narrowed her eyes. "Some kind of tabloid-hungry squatcher out to make an easy buck on the World Wide Web from my misfortune? I'm not interested in lunacy or publicity, thank you very much."

"No, I didn't mean—" Lucy quickly shoved the notebook into her overstuffed bag. "I'm not a squatcher, honest." She sensed that the old woman's patience was rapidly wearing thin. "How about lights in the sky?" she blurted out in desperation. "Have you or Mrs Stricks seen any UFOs?"

She regretted saying it immediately.

The Other Mrs Stricks's cheeks flushed crimson. "U. F. Os," she enunciated slowly. The cuckoo clock began to chime. "I have neither the time nor the energy for this today, Sladan." The old woman glared into space, seemingly lost in thought. "I have nothing more to say. Now, please go."

Lucy mentally kicked herself as she gathered up her bag. "Look, something weird is going on around here. I can't be the only one who's noticed." She stood. "I'm sorry I bothered you. I hope Mrs Stricks comes back soon."

Frustrated and dejected, Lucy slunk out of the cottage. *That went well.* A dark cloud drifted over the sun and the breeze disappeared, the forest eerily still.

Momentarily out of ideas and certain she wouldn't be welcome at the search party, Lucy headed down the road back towards school. She paused when she heard the sound of footsteps behind her. As soon as she whipped around to look, the sound stopped.

Was there something moving in the bushes or was it just her imagination? "Who's there?" No answer. She picked up a rock and threw it as hard as she could into the foliage.

"Ow!" yelped a familiar voice. Milo popped out from behind a huckleberry bush, hands raised in surrender. "OK, you caught me."

"What the flying fart?" said Lucy. "You're *following* me?"

"I saw you sneak off campus," he said. "I figured wherever you were headed was bound to be more interesting than raccoon puppets."

"Am I supposed to be flattered?" she asked.

"I don't suppose you would be." Milo stepped out on to the path. He wore a tan trench coat over a blue button-down shirt and a pair of khakis, all of which were, again, unsuitable for the outdoors. "I heard that the English teacher went missing," he said, concerned. "I like her class. She seems clever."

"How do you know that if you ditched school when I did?"

"My dad told me about it this morning."

The picture thief. "How'd he hear about it?"

"He stays well informed. He joined the search party this morning. Who was that lady you were visiting?"

"That's the Other Mrs Stricks. I thought she might know something about what happened."

"Did she?"

"Less than nothing." Lucy kicked a pebble. "It was worth a shot, I guess."

"Well," said Milo, "maybe this will cheer you up." He reached into his coat pocket and pulled out the digital camera his father had confiscated the night before. It was now attached to a chunky telephoto lens like Lucy had seen in spy movies.

"No way," she gawped. "You got your camera back!"

Milo ceremoniously placed the device into her outstretched hands. "My computer is sadly no more, but the camera is fine. In other news, I know what I'm getting for my birthday."

Lucy draped the strap around her neck. "Are the pictures still on here?"

"Yes," said Milo tentatively, "the pictures are there, but…"

"But what?" she said, flipping through the thumbnails. "Did you look at them?"

"Of course. I went straight to number two forty-nine, like you said. But…"

"What's the problem? Did your dad delete the picture? If that laserbrain deleted the picture, I swear—"

"Laserbrain? Really?" He scowled. "Look,

the pictures are all there, it's just…" He took a deep breath. "Bigwoof's not."

Lucy stared at him blankly. Thunder rumbled in the distance. A soft drizzle began to fall, raindrops pattering gently on the trees around them.

"I looked at every single photograph," Milo insisted, "but, well, see for yourself."

Lucy found picture two forty-nine. It was the right photo, but something was wrong. She zoomed into the spot where the creature had been. Now she saw nothing but shadows and trees. Suddenly she was unsure of what to do with her hands, or what hands were, or why hers felt so numb.

"I had a chat with my dad at breakfast," said Milo, "and he had a suggestion."

Lucy gave him a death stare.

"Isn't it possible," he continued, a tad too brightly, "that after being struck by lightning, not getting enough sleep and looking at literally hundreds of photographs, you, kind of, maybe, saw what you wanted to see?"

Lucy noted that he had stepped out of punching range. "I was not imagining things."

She returned her attention to number two forty-nine, the photograph that could have proved the existence of the supernatural, the picture that could have changed the world.

Milo's head snapped around. "Did you hear something?"

"Hear what?" Lucy clicked frantically through more photos on the camera, but Bigwoof was nowhere to be found. A million and one thoughts ran through her mind, none of them kind.

Then she heard it too – a rustling in the bushes behind Milo. *Sweet baby corn, now what?*

A dark, furry creature emerged from the shadows between two ferns, heading straight for them.

"Oh wow," said Milo, pointing to the cutest, cuddliest thing he had ever seen. "It's a baby bear!"

Lucy's muscles tensed. *Oh no.* "Back away,

Fish," she warned.

He bent down and reached out a hand for the bear to sniff. "Hey there, little guy." He beamed back at Lucy. "This is so neat. I've never seen a bear up close before. Take a picture, will you?"

"That's not a bear," Lucy hissed.

"What do you call it then?" he asked. "It's not a pup."

"Fish."

"Cub! It's a little baby bear cub."

"Fish!" She grabbed his shoulder and pointed him towards the trees behind the cub, where Milo now saw something big, and hairy, and full of teeth. "*That's* a bear."

CHAPTER 6

Beasts and Bigwoofs

The black bear rose to her full, towering height and let out a bellowing roar. Had Lucy been able to speak, she could have informed Milo that mother bears are called sows.

Milo leapt away from the cub and clung to Lucy's side. "Should we run?" he whispered.

"No," said Lucy. "Back up slowly and don't make any sudden moves." She held him by the elbow and led him gently away.

The sow dropped to all fours, snuffled and pawed the dirt. For a brief moment, Lucy thought that would be the end of it. Then Milo tripped on the hem of his oversized coat. He flailed and yelped before Lucy caught him. The mother bear bellowed again, then charged.

"Run!" Lucy squealed, gripping Milo's hand.

They ran. The bear was at their heels in an instant. Everything felt like it was happening in slow motion. Lucy yanked Milo over a log, down a crumbling slope and into a gully. It took the mother bear just a moment to reorient herself to the chase, but it was enough for them to gain some distance. It almost looked as if they were going to escape when they hit a slick of mud that sent them slide-tumbling down an embankment.

After rolling and bumping for what seemed like a painful eternity, they sprawled on to the dank forest floor. Lucy tried to stand, but her ankle gave out and she fell to her knees.

Milo was worse off. Head ringing, he writhed on the ground, wheezing. A blow to the sternum had knocked the wind out of him. He gasped for air as he rolled over on to his back.

Lucy could hear the thudding, grunting

approach of the mother bear rushing towards them. She threw her body over Milo's in a clumsy but daring attempt at heroism, nailing him in the nose with her elbow. Now he was bleeding everywhere.

Oh glob oh glob oh glob! Lucy closed her eyes and dug her nails into Milo's trench coat.

Suddenly, she heard the sickening THUD of meat against meat as the bear's roar turned into a howl of surprise. Lucy sat up like a meerkat on the plain.

The sow was sprawled out on its back, moaning in confusion. Crouched between the bear and the children, so close Lucy could smell its sweat, was a heaving humanoid beast, its dark, scraggly hair bristling over tautly muscled shoulders.

"BIGWOOF!" Lucy shrieked. She clasped her hands over her mouth.

The grotesque, blunt-faced giant turned to roar in her face, its eyes like black marbles, its pointy, snaggled teeth like those of an anglerfish.

So this is how I die, thought Lucy. *I can live with that.*

Behind Bigwoof, the bear scrambled to its feet and pawed the ground again, gearing up for battle.

Without a glance behind, Bigwoof leapt skyward and flipped around in mid-air, landing in a crouch in front of the panicked animal. The bear swung its heavy paw like a club and knocked the monster, CHONK, into a knotty tree.

Bigwoof lunged at the sow and the pair rolled, mashing and gnashing, across the forest floor, flattening the foliage in their wake.

"Bigwoof is saving us," Lucy muttered in disbelief. She glanced down at Milo, who was curled up in the undergrowth with his hands over his wounded face. "Look, Fish, look!"

Gasping for air and choking on the blood gushing from his nose, Milo rolled over and raised himself up on all fours, squinting at the commotion. "Cool," Lucy swore she could hear him say, just before he collapsed face-down in a puddle of mud.

Lucy realised with an ecstatic pang that Milo's camera was still hanging around her neck. She held it up, taking as many pictures as she could. "Do you see?" she said. "I can't believe this is happening. This is amazing. Are you seeing this? Fish? Do you see?"

"What do you mean you're not sure what you saw?!" Lucy gestured wildly at the dozen footprints she had filled with plaster and left to dry on the sloped forest floor. The beastly fight was long over, ending with both creatures disappearing into the woods.

"Bigwoof rammed the bear here," Lucy pointed towards a tangled patch of brambles, "and the bear was like 'whoa, what the heck' and it stumbled over *here*." She ran around to give Milo an impression of the beastly struggle.

He picked up one of the plaster casts Lucy had made while they had waited for his nosebleed to stop. "Huh." He scratched some dried blood off his nostril.

She grabbed the print out of his hands and examined it again. She had never seen a foot like this before. It was incredible – as big as her forearm and twice as wide, with long, clawless toes. It certainly didn't resemble the human-looking "Bigfoot prints" they sold at Smiley's Souvenirs down on Main Street.

"Well, maybe if somebody hadn't punched me in the face..." said Milo.

"For the last time," Lucy insisted, "it was my elbow and it was an accident."

"Then maybe I would've been able to see whatever it was you saw."

She scowled. "Well, maybe you deserved a bloody nose for spying on me anyway."

"*Touché.*" Milo held out his hands in a gesture of peace.

His shirt was untucked and splattered with blood, his trousers were stained with mud and his hair was sticking up on one side. Lucy thought it was an improvement.

Milo picked up the camera and flicked through the pictures Lucy had taken moments ago. "I still don't know how you managed not to get a single decent picture of the bear fight."

"It was that stupid lens you put on it," she moaned. "It made everything blurry." She lay down on the ground and stared up at the yellowing leaves of the canopy above. "I give up," she said. "I'm never moving from this spot."

"That sounds reasonable," Milo deadpanned. "What's this?" He squinted at one of the blurry pictures. "There's a pink splotch on one of the brownish blobs."

"I dunno," said Lucy. "It's probably my finger." She could feel muddy water soaking through the seat of her jeans. *Perfect.*

"I don't think so," said Milo. "This is pink-pink, not pinky-pink."

"I'm starting to think you just like the way words sound," Lucy whimpered.

Milo squinted into the trees. "Which way did

you say the bear went?"

Lucy pointed.

Milo gathered up most of the plaster prints and shoved them into Lucy's dirt-caked backpack. "OK, grumpy," he said. "Up 'n' at 'em."

They trudged down the gully past a trickling waterfall until they reached a dense grove of wizened sticky pines.

Lucy spotted an indented splotch of mud. "There's another footprint!" She took out a print-making kit and mixed up the last of the plaster.

Milo examined the distinctive trees that gave the town its name. Their long, sharp needles were an unusual deep blue. He reached out a finger and touched the glistening black ooze dripping lazily down a twisty grey trunk. When he pulled back, a thin strand of sap followed and then broke away, hovering in the air for a moment before folding back into the rest of the goo.

"These trees are quite unique," he said. "Did

you know they've got the stickiest sap on the planet?"

"Yeah, we did a project about that in kindergarten," said Lucy. She shook the mixture and poured the milkshake-thick plaster into the footprint. "The sap's fireproof and waterproof too."

"Hey, look." Milo noticed something stuck to a stunted pine at the back of the grove. "It's that pink thing I saw in the picture."

Lucy hopped to her good foot and wiped her plaster-covered fingers on her sweatshirt, leaving dove-like streaks of white. She hobbled towards him as Milo pulled a woollen object free from the tangled trees. It was covered in mud, sap and pine needles. He held it out. It looked like a small striped blanket.

Lucy paled as she pointed to a dark-red stain on the edge of the grey and pink wool. "Is that blood?"

"I hope not," Milo swallowed.

He offered one end to Lucy and the pair held it

out at full length.

Lucy gasped. "This is the shawl the Other Mrs Stricks was wearing." She felt as though her stomach was slowly filling with iced water.

"Maybe she came outside to look for her wife," said Milo. "Do you think the bear got her?"

"Or something worse. Come on," urged Lucy.

They clambered back up the gully, past the waterfall, and raced along the path all the way to the Strickses' log cabin. Lucy thundered up the front steps, knocking one of the owl statues from its perch. She ran through the open door and into the house, red-faced and shaking.

The place was utterly destroyed. The shelves of oddities were smashed, snow globes lying in glittery puddles on the wood floor. The glass coffee table was shattered, along with the many empty mugs that had sat upon it. Lucy ran to the kitchen, where the bubbling brew lay splattered all over the linoleum. She turned off the gas burner and went back to the living room.

Milo slid to a stop and dropped the heavy

backpack at Lucy's side. He put a hand on the back of the love seat and tried to catch his breath. "Ew!" He jerked his hand back. His fingers were covered in some kind of colourless ooze.

"What is that stuff?" She noticed a globby puddle on the seat of the shredded floral armchair. "There's slime all over the place." Lucy took a plastic bag out of her backpack and scraped some of the gunk into it.

"It's like that stuff that was on your shoes when you got struck by lightning," said Milo. Grimacing, he wiped his hand on his shirt. "This looks bad, Lucy," said Milo. "Really bad."

Lucy packed the slime sample into her bag and searched the room for signs of what had happened. The curtains over the front window had been torn, the metal rod bent in the centre and dangling from one side.

Lucy felt the tattered edges of the drapes. "These look like claw marks."

Milo's face fell as he looked out the window. "Uh, Lucy?" he said.

"Son of a scab licker," she muttered. "Now what?"

Together, they stared out the window at the scariest thing they had seen all day. Headed down the dirt path straight towards the cabin was the search party for Mrs Stricks. Leading the way were their parents.

CHAPTER 7

Bigfoot Breakthrough

Grounded. Like, seriously grounded. Lucy's parents had previously used the word when punishing her, but never before had she actually been completely and utterly cut off from the outside world. *All because of a harmless and perfectly legal (probably) investigation into dangerous paranormal activity.*

Until further notice, Lucy was denied television, visitors, the Internet, her backpack, reading for fun, writing her memoirs, messaging in any fashion and talking on the phone. She was to spend her lunch period in the science room grading papers with her mother and not in the cafeteria with Tex and, more specifically, "that Fisher kid".

Adding to her troubles, Lucy may have appeared to overreact at the Strickses' cabin when Mr Fisher had "innocently" reached for her evidence-filled backpack.

"Get your hands off me, KGB!" she had screeched at the top of her lungs as she tried to twist the bag out of Mr Fisher's hands.

She kicked him hard in the shin. He doubled over but didn't let go.

"Lucita Alvera Galena Sladan!" yelled Miranda Sladan, furiously pushing her way through the *What are those kids doing here?*s and *What happened here?*s of the bewildered search party.

Lucy was about to lose her grip on her precious pack when her mother brusquely yanked it away from her and an equally surprised Mr Fisher.

"I'll take this, thank you very much," said Miranda. She looked Mr Fisher coolly in the eye, threw the backpack over her shoulders and marched out the front door.

Mr Fisher said nothing, his face a stone mask.

Without meeting Fisher's gaze, Silas placed an arm around his daughter and gently guided her towards the front door of the crowded cabin.

Lucy glanced back over her shoulder. Milo was on the other side of the living room being poked and prodded by someone with a stethoscope. His stepmother was on the phone, looking very displeased. Lucy figured it was probably all the dried blood on his face. She had the feeling it would be some time before they saw each other again.

Early the following morning, when everyone had calmed down a bit, the Sladan family met in the kitchen for pancakes.

"You think locking me up is going to stop people from disappearing?" Lucy argued. "I'm the only person who's seen what's out there. People are in danger, for cripes sake."

She reached across the island countertop for

the coffee pot and poured herself a cup. Her father immediately snatched it from her hand.

Silas drank the coffee and sat on the stool across from her. "I hate to break it to you, kid," he said, "but you are twelve years old. The fate of the world does not rest on your shoulders."

"You told the sheriff what you thought you saw," said Miranda. "What else can you do?" She pointed at Lucy with the spatula she was using to flip pancakes. "It's time for you to come back down to earth. Deal with the microcosm you actually live in."

"What's a microcosm?" asked Willow, looking up from the funny pages.

"Nobody is taking me seriously," Lucy whined.

"Nobody is taking your *Bigfoot sighting* seriously," Miranda emphasised. She wiped her forehead, leaving a streak of flour, and slid two steaming pancakes on to Lucy's plate. "Does this surprise you?"

"Will you at least look at the slime I found at

the Strickses' place?"

"That stuff could be anything, Luce," said Miranda. "Just let it go."

"Please!" Lucy begged.

"I'll think about it!" Miranda took a plate of pancakes into the living room to eat in peace.

"A microcosm is a tiny universe," Silas said to Willow. He read the front page of the local newspaper, *The Sticky Times*, which reported that stores were now running out of bottled water, canned goods and ammunition. "Boy howdy," he whistled. "Things are starting to feel freaky around here."

Tell me about it. Lucy begrudgingly took a bite of her delicious breakfast and chewed in silence. It always came down to proof. Until she had some, nobody was going to listen. *Nobody*.

By the following weekend, time had begun to lose all meaning. Having been stuck indoors for nine whole days, Lucy learned that in prison it's the little things that drive you mad.

After spending three hours writing a report on the mimic octopus for her mother's class (by hand, like some kind of Neanderthal), she paused to shake out a wrist cramp.

Errol sat up drowsily from his spot by the desk and nudged her fingers until she scratched him under the chin. "What's up, buddy? You bored?"

Errol sneezed.

"You and me both."

There was a heavy FLUMP outside the closed bedroom door.

"Hello?" asked Lucy. No one answered.

I thought I'm not allowed visitors…

She slumped across the attic, hopping over a pile of books, and opened the door. There was a My Little Pony duffel bag sitting on the landing.

Huh?

"Whatcha doin'?" said a voice from above.

Lucy looked up. Her little sister sat cross-legged in the rafters, grinning like a gap-toothed Cheshire cat.

"What's in the bag?" Lucy asked suspiciously. The last time Willow had given her a package it had contained a live garter snake.

"Nothing venomous," said Willow unhelpfully.

Lucy picked up the heavier-than-expected sack and dragged it into her room. Willow swung down and trotted after her.

Errol sniffed the duffel, snorted, then lay down on the beanbag looking disappointed.

Well, it's not food. It couldn't be another care package from Tex. He had cycled over earlier in the week with a box containing pickled fish and stewed deer meat from his father's deli, and some very welcome (and immediately confiscated) graphic novels.

Lucy sat on the rumpled bed and unzipped the bag. *No flippin' way.* "The footprint casts!"

Willow crawled on the floor towards Errol. "They were hidden in Mom's closet."

"You stole these for me? Thanks, Will."

"I owed you for collecting those owl pellets over the summer. Also, your friends said you needed them or you'd go crazy."

"Friends, plural?" asked Lucy.

"My thoughts exactly," Willow snickered. "That new kid you commit crimes with has been hanging out with Tex all week."

"Without me?" said Lucy. "That's disturbing."

"Agreed." Willow affectionately smooshed Errol's face between her hands. "Why can't you have normal friends?"

"Why can't you have human friends?" Lucy retorted.

Willow let Errol lick her entire face.

Lucy emptied the bag on the bed and picked up one of the casts. She ran her fingers along the surface of the mysterious creature's footprint. *Incredible*.

"Are you officially calling yourself a squatcher yet?" said Willow.

Lucy flung the empty bag at her sister's head.

Willow ducked. "Gee, you're grouchy when you're grounded. Why don't you talk to your new boyfriend about it?"

"OK, I'm actually going to murder you." Lucy balled up a fist.

"I'm serious," said Willow. "He's downstairs."

"What?" The blood drained from Lucy's face. She looked out the attic window. Sure enough, an unfamiliar silver sports car was parked in the driveway. She skidded across the floor, skipped across the landing and bounded down the stairs.

Mr Fisher and his son sat on the worn leather couch in the living room. Lucy's dad sat in the rocking chair, while her mom was perched on a stool she had brought in from the kitchen. Everyone stopped talking as soon as Lucy appeared.

"Speak of the devil," said Mr Fisher. He smiled and gestured for Lucy to have a seat.

She sat on the floor next to the coffee table. Milo greeted her with a nod.

"We were just having a chat with Mr Fisher," said Silas.

"Long overdue, I'm afraid," Milo's father chimed in, "considering you're one of our top men on the factory floor, as I understand it."

"That's kind of you to say, sir." Silas looked quite pleased.

Mr Fisher cleared his throat. "I came here to talk about Milo. You see, I just can't abide seeing him upset."

Lucy glanced at Milo, who was sipping a glass of milk.

"My son means everything to me," Fisher continued, "and as I'm sure you've gathered, he's quite fond of your daughter. I must admit, after meeting this bright, spirited young lady the other day, I can certainly understand why."

Silas smiled while Miranda pursed her lips.

"Milo's a good kid," Fisher placed a hand on his son's shoulder, "but like his mother, he tends to get a little carried away sometimes. I'm sure you folks have no experience with *that*." He raised an eyebrow in Lucy's direction.

Silas burst into laughter.

Lucy's eye twitched.

Mr Fisher smoothed his lustrous red tie.

"Now, I know things got a little hairy last week, but I think we can all agree that these kids had good intentions. They wanted to help find their teacher. A noble venture, if ever there was one."

"Oh, I'm not sure about that," said Miranda. She narrowed her eyes at Lucy. "Skipping school and running around the woods like maniacs in the middle of a rash of unexplained disappearances shows an *astounding* lack of judgement."

Mr Fisher nodded. "Miranda," he said, his fingers forming a tepee, "I can certainly appreciate your concern. Sticky Pines is a quaint little town and I'm sure you're used to things running smoothly around here. And while we should certainly take the recent disappearances seriously –" he put a hand on his heart – "from what I understand, all signs point to a series of unfortunate, but unconnected, misadventures. In this case, our children have stumbled upon the latest culprit: an overprotective mother bear. Simple as that."

Lucy dug her nails into her palms so hard she

nearly drew blood. Milo smirked as if he could sense how hard she was fighting the urge to scream "BIGWOOF ISN'T A BEAR!"

"Hmm," said Miranda. "Is it really as simple as that?" She tapped her knees thoughtfully. "You know, Lucy collected a sample of some sort of slime at the Strickses' cabin on the day of the latest disappearance."

"Slime?" Mr Fisher chortled. "Is that a scientific term?"

"It's an accurate description," said Miranda. "Clear, gelatinous slime. The police didn't know what to make of it. I brought it to the school lab and took a closer look."

Lucy perked up. *She actually did it.* She had never been prouder of her mother.

"What a creative use of educational resources." Mr Fisher's smile didn't reach his eyes.

"It's an organic substance," Miranda continued. "A secretion from an animal, I would guess. But I discovered something rather unusual about it."

Lucy was listening intently. *Now, this is getting interesting.*

"Nucralose," said Miranda.

Nucralose?

Mr Fisher narrowed his eyes. "Pardon me?"

"The substance contained a significant amount of the new sweetener made by your company." Miranda cocked her head. "Can you think of any reason for this?"

Lucy sensed a crackle of tension as Mr Fisher shifted in his seat, pondering her mother's words.

"That's a fair question," he said at last, "and one that I'll be more than happy to have the team at my facility look into. I can't thank you enough for bringing this to my attention. Would you mind talking me through your findings?"

"Of course," said Miranda.

Silas put a hand on Lucy's head. "Why don't you squirts head up to the attic?"

"No thanks. I wanna hear more about the slime," said Lucy.

"Are you saying you don't want to spend time

with a non-blood relative for the first time in a week?" said Miranda.

"Ugh, fine." Lucy stood up. *Just when it was getting good.*

She led Milo through the kitchen and into the back hallway.

"Hey," Milo smiled, his hands in his peacoat pockets. "For a minute, I was worried I'd never see you again."

"Me too," said Lucy. "I can't believe your dad went to bat for you like this. That's so … nice?"

"Yeah. It took a lot of strategic sulking," said Milo. "Last week, he was considering sending me to his old boarding school. In Kansas. Supposedly, he loved the place." He stuck a finger down his throat. "I like your house, by the way." He stepped on a floorboard. "Nice and creaky."

"Thanks," said Lucy. She wondered what he would think of her untidy room.

Up in the attic, the sun was setting. A soft pink glow filtered through the window. The room was already occupied when Milo and Lucy arrived.

"Greetings, jailbird." Tex was sitting in the rolling desk chair. He held up an opened jar of pickled herring Lucy somehow hadn't gotten around to eating. "I hope you don't mind. I missed lunch."

Willow sat on the floor arranging the plaster footprint casts in a circle in the middle of the room. She pointed at Tex. "Does *it* have an off switch?"

"*You* let me in," Tex retorted.

All my worlds are colliding. Lucy slumped into the orange beanbag chair. "Is this some sort of intervention?"

Tex spread his arms wide. "Think of it as an invitation," he said, "to return to the real world."

"Says the Dungeon Master," Milo laughed. He smoothed the comforter on Lucy's dishevelled bed before sitting down.

"I do not get my realities confused," said Tex. "Besides, studies show that people who enjoy role-playing games do not get knocked unconscious, struck by lightning or nearly drown as often as kids who hang out with Lucy Sladan."

Lucy stuck out her tongue.

"Cheer up," said Milo. "I brought you something." He reached into his coat pocket and pulled out a large plaster footprint, the one they had left behind when they found the Other Mrs Stricks's shawl.

Lucy sprang up from her seat and took the cast. "You went back?"

"I brought Tex along for protection," he joked. "And also to show me where to go."

Tex cracked open Lucy's can of reindeer meat with a Swiss army knife. "Do you see the size of those claws?" he said. "You guys are lucky to be breathing."

"Claws?" asked Lucy, examining the new print with keen interest. "The print I saw before didn't have any."

"Looks almost like a troll foot," said Tex.

Milo groaned and loosened his grey tie. "I

thought you were the rational one."

"Trolls exist," Tex pointed his meat-filled fork at Milo, "but they only live in Siberia. I saw one once when I was small."

"Are you sure you didn't just see a mirror?" said Willow. She ducked as a glob of meat sailed over her head and splatted on the floor.

Errol selflessly trotted over to clean up the mess.

"What was it you guys wanted to tell me?" asked Lucy.

Tex scraped up the last of the reindeer meat. "We think Bigwoof is a grolar bear."

"A what?" said Lucy.

"It's what you get when a grizzly bear falls in love with a polar bear," said Willow.

Lucy did not look impressed.

"We googled some prints for comparison," said Milo. "It's our closest bet, and it could easily explain the bear fight you saw. It's an animal that doesn't belong here. It would have to be sick or desperate to come this far south." He clapped his hands. "Boom. Bigwoof."

Lucy re-examined the footprint in her hands. The long, menacing claws did resemble those of a grizzly, or even a grolar bear for all she knew. As more time passed, she found it harder to remember the details of the creature – the precise colour of its fur, the length of its teeth, its height; everything blurred together. *If only I had that stupid picture.*

"Can I see it?" asked Willow.

Lucy sullenly handed over the cast. Willow added it to the circle of footprints on the floor.

"What are you doing with those anyway?" Lucy asked.

"Putting them in order," Willow responded.

In order? Lucy adjusted her glasses and walked around to get a better view. *Wait a minute.* A chill ran from her shoulders to her fingertips. "Whoa."

"What now?" said Tex. He squinted at the layout on the floor.

"It's changing," said Lucy. She walked slowly

around the circle, pointing at each print in turn. "Look. The creature's foot and claws are growing longer over time."

Tex examined the nearest footprint. It was big and fat like a bear's, but without any claws. As the prints moved around the circle, the foot grew longer, the toes further apart, a grisly set of raptor talons emerging at last.

"No way," said Tex. "What the heck *is* that thing?"

"Come on, guys." Milo pressed his palms against his eye sockets. "I thought we agreed it was a mangy bear."

"Well, frankly," said Lucy, "if your dad hadn't messed with that picture, we'd be able to answer this question once and for all."

"I told you," snapped Milo. "My dad wouldn't do that."

"OK," said Lucy, hands on her hips, "let's settle this. Do you have your camera?"

Milo looked dubious but pulled it out of his coat pocket.

"Give it to Tex," said Lucy.

"Why?" asked Milo.

"He's a Photoshop expert."

"He put my head on a T-rex's body once," said Willow. "It looked real."

"Come," said Tex. "Trust me with your expensive machinery." He took the camera from a reluctant Milo and searched through some of the photos. "Why are there pictures of Lucy and the Other Mrs Stricks on here?"

"Never mind those," said Milo, his cheeks pink.

"It's picture number two forty-nine," said Lucy.

Tex plugged the camera into Lucy's computer. They all watched as the images loaded onscreen. Tex scrolled around carefully, zooming in and out, grunting now and then. After several tense minutes, he spoke. "Well. I hate to say this, but Lucy is right."

"What?" said Milo.

"I *knew* it!" Lucy did a victory dance.

"This picture," Tex declared, "has been Shooped."

"Shooped?" asked Milo.

"Altered. Modified. Messed with," Lucy explained. She skipped over to the desk as she ran out of synonyms. Milo tentatively followed.

"You see here?" said Tex. He pointed at the spot where Lucy had seen the creature. "If you look closely," he scrolled down, "you can see that this dark, leafy area has been copied and pasted," he scrolled back over, "on top of this area." He demonstrated where the edges of the cut-and-paste job were faintly blurred. "It is quite sophisticated work," he added, impressed.

"Let me see." Milo pushed Tex out of the chair and sat.

"Knock, knock!" It was Miranda, calling up from the foot of the attic stairs.

Jolted, Lucy grabbed the beanbag chair and threw it on top of the footprints she wasn't supposed to have, then awkwardly sat on it.

Miranda poked her head in the room. "I'm

going to pretend it's a good sign it's so quiet up here."

Everyone but Milo looked up as the three parents entered the room.

"Mr and Mrs Sladan, it is so good to see you." Tex greeted them with his arms wide. "Your moustache is looking exceptionally full today, Mr S."

"Why, thank you, Alexei," said Silas. "Did you let him in?" he asked his wife.

"Have a seat, kids," said Miranda.

"We've got some news," said Silas.

Tex sat next to Willow.

"Bad news?" asked Lucy.

"Good news, actually," her father replied. "Also better news, and even some fantastic news.

"That's a lot of good news," said Lucy suspiciously.

"First," said Miranda, "we just learned that your father is up for a promotion at work." She beamed at Silas, who looked like he couldn't quite believe his good fortune. "He's going to be a supervisor at Nu Co., which means longer hours, but a raise in salary."

Mr Fisher offered Silas a happy handshake.

"What's the better news?" Willow asked.

Milo looked away from the computer screen and stared at his father.

"As a gift to the people of Sticky Pines in the wake of so much turmoil," said Mr Fisher, "the Nu Corporation would like to donate a day of fun. We're throwing a carnival. With games, rides and all the state-of-the-art Nu Co. food products the town can eat."

"A carnival?" said Lucy.

"Food?" said Tex.

"And the best part?" said Miranda, smiling at her eldest daughter. "You get to go too."

"That's the fantastic news," said Silas. "You are officially ungrounded." He nodded at his boss. "You can thank Mr Fisher for that. He's a very persuasive man."

Lucy looked from her cheerful mother to her sheepishly grinning father, to the sickeningly self-satisfied photoshopping Mr Fisher. *Something's very wrong here.*

"Wow," she said, trying to look pleased. "Just, wow."

"That's right, kiddo," said Mr Fisher, a glint in his eye. "Come next weekend, Nu Co. is taking over Sticky Pines."

CHAPTER 8

Sunshine and Other Portents of Doom

It was the day of Fisher's festival, and for the first time in a week, there was no rain. Lucy took this to be a dark omen.

"Come on, sport, get your shoes on," said Silas. He had finished loading the last of his gear into the van and was now tapping his foot as he waited for his sluggish daughter to get ready. "I don't like being up at seven on a Saturday any more than you do."

Lucy sat at the bottom of the stairs, staring at what looked like a wailing face in the grain of the hardwood floor. Normally, she was first in line when a carnival came to town. She loved the rides and the games and the ridiculous portions of fried food. But Fisher's carnival was different. For one thing, it was called "The First Annual Nu Co. Par-T in Da Pines".

Ugh.

"Your shoes are tied, well done," said Silas, utilising every ounce of patience he could muster. "Now, stand up."

Lucy reached for her overstuffed backpack on the stair behind her.

"Nuh-uh," said Silas. "I told you. You're not dragging that thing around all day."

Everything Lucy needed to collect and process evidence was in that bag. Everything.

"Leave. The. Bag."

Outside, Miranda honked the car horn.

"But, Father," Lucy said in her most rational voice, "I have a really bad feeling about—"

"Enough," said Silas firmly. "Let's go." He guided Lucy by the shoulders out to the idling green minivan.

Resigned to her fate, Lucy buckled up and

rested her head against a battered guitar case. She turned towards her sister, half asleep on the other side of the food-stained back seat. "There's something fishy about this carnival."

"Yeah, you mentioned that." Willow pulled her faux coonskin cap over her eyes. "About a zillion times."

"And we're off!" said Miranda, shifting the minivan into gear.

Silas turned up the radio as they ambled down the road out of their north-west neighbourhood, meandering along the Ungula River, past the schoolhouse, towards Wildberry Fairground on the other side of the valley.

Lucy pensively watched the trees fly past the moon roof, their sun-dappled leaves turning red, yellow and orange as the autumn deepened.

Things with Milo had been weird since the day he and his dad had visited. Tex had finally confirmed what Lucy already knew to be true: Mr Fisher had altered the picture of Bigwoof, for reasons that were still unclear. She should be feeling elated, or at least vindicated. Milo, however, was clearly miserable, and Lucy didn't know how to fix it.

She had only seen him once since then, on the way to the cafeteria, when he had abruptly excused himself to go "catch up on homework" in the library. *Right.* She wished he'd at least hang around long enough for her to tell him how dumb his polo shirt looked, or something.

The trees parted and the van emerged at the top of a grassy hill dotted with crimson huckleberry bushes, overlooking a vast meadow that served as the local fairground. Dozens of events were held out there every year, like the "Cheese Rolling Races" and the "Big Crater Quilting Festival", but Lucy had never seen such an elaborate set-up as there was today.

Garish gaming stalls, colourful vendors and flashy rides sprawled out kaleidoscopically across the meadow, including a Ferris wheel so tall Lucy's stomach churned just looking at it.

All this, just for us?

Her skin prickled as she spotted a large banner hanging above the front entrance. A smiling clown with black diamond tears beckoned the crowd with a white-gloved hand to "Join The Fun!" Lucy could practically hear its demented laughter.

Adding to her sense of unease, she noticed about a dozen inflatable white structures with red crosses scattered across the grounds. *Are those medical tents? Sticky Pines is taking safety very seriously these days...*

"This looks amazing," Silas exclaimed. He turned to the kids in the back seat. "You guys are gonna have a blast."

"Us?" said Lucy. "You're the excited ones."

Miranda raised a thin eyebrow in the rear-view mirror as she caught Lucy's eye. "Excuse me, missy. We're volunteers. I'll be spending most of my day counting tickets. Your dad will be glued to the bandstand. I probably won't even get to ride the Gravitator." She sighed. "I love centrifugal force."

"I know you do, babe." Silas placed his arm around Miranda's shoulders.

I can't deal with this today.

Willow took her raccoon hat by the tail and swung it around excitedly.

"What are you so worked up about?" asked Lucy.

"I'm on a mission," said Willow. "I'm gonna win a prize at every game at this fair."

"Every single one?" said Silas. "That's impossible. Those games are all rigged, Will."

"I looked up all the tricks." Willow grinned slyly.

"And they cost money to play," said Miranda.

"I have money," said Willow.

"Since when?" asked Silas.

"She's been dismantling owl pellets and selling rodent skulls on the Internet," said Lucy. "She uses Tex's brother Stan's bank account."

"He charges a small fee, but it's pretty reasonable," said Willow.

"Is that even legal?" asked Miranda.

"Yup," said Willow. "As long as the bones aren't from an endangered species."

Miranda pulled into a parking space near the ticket booth. "All right, everybody out," she said. "Whoever unloads the most stuff in two minutes wins their song of choice from The Sticky Six."

The Sticky Six was the name of Silas's rock band. It had only four members.

"Ready, set, go!" Miranda shouted.

Willow flew out of the vehicle before Lucy could even unbuckle her seatbelt.

Lucy hopped out of the van and let the sliding door rumble shut behind her. That's when she saw them – two men dressed in kitschy clothing, with colourful wigs and doofy face make-up.

"Clowns," she muttered. "Of course Fisher hired clowns."

"You're still afraid of clowns?" Silas grunted as he set a hefty amplifier on a dolly with a WHUMP. "Aren't you a little old for that?"

Lucy shivered. Bigwoof, whatever it was, was

one thing. Clowns were an entirely different kind of monstrosity. On the list of things that terrified her, clowns came just after spiders and kids who make "unboxing" videos.

"Finished," Willow cried triumphantly. She jumped on to her father's back, throwing her arms around his neck like a rhesus monkey. "I call … 'Eye of the Tiger'!"

"All right, you little girl-illa," said Silas, "'Eye of the Tiger' it is."

Willow hopped to the ground and ran around the van in a fit of victory.

This is going to be a very long day.

POW!

After throwing dart number twelve, Willow obliterated a third balloon into shards of flabby green rubber.

Finally.

A bald man with earrings and fully tattooed arms handed Willow a stuffed strawberry wearing shorts and sunglasses.

She sceptically regarded her hard-won prize. "What's this supposed to be?"

"It's a fruit," said the dude.

"It's an anthropomorphic fruit," said Lucy.

The carnival worker blinked dully.

"It's wearing clothes like a person," Lucy clarified.

"*You're* an animorphic fruit," said Willow. She handed her sister her latest trophy.

Lucy took the beach-ready berry in her arms, where it joined two tiny teddy bears, an inflatable shark and a wide-mouthed Muppet that shed fuchsia fur all over her black wolf moon T-shirt.

"Don't forget to try the new Nu Co. products served all over the fair," the dude intoned, repeating the pitch Lucy and Willow had heard again and again from the other carnival workers. He shuffled over to another customer – a woman wearing a furry green hat adorned with the Nu Co. insignia. She held a fistful of cash and a bucket-sized serving of Nu Co. Cola.

"Time for a Sticky treat!" chirped Willow, echoing the ubiquitous catchphrase plastered all over the festival.

She led a sullen Lucy to the nearest vendor and bought a bag of blue fluff labelled "NuCotton Candy".

"Stretchy," said Willow, pulling the wad apart like spider's silk. She shoved a clump in her mouth.

Lucy felt her stomach rumble. "Oof, I'm hungry."

"Have some," Willow offered.

"I want real food."

"Suit yourself." Willow licked her fingers with a turquoise tongue. "There's a frozen banana stand over by where Dad's playing."

"Yeah, I saw," said Lucy, "but it's surrounded by a bunch of clowns."

"I hate clowns," said a Russian-inflected voice from behind them.

Lucy brightened up as Tex fist-bumped her shoulder.

"You cannot avoid the clowns," he said. "They are everywhere. I saw one on stilts, terrorising people by the Ferris wheel. I wanted to pour black salt in its footprints. You need a hand with that junk?" He gestured at the prizes overflowing in Lucy's arms.

"Thanks." She sighed with relief and handed them over.

Her stomach rumbled. "Let's go to the banana stand. We can stop by The Sticky Six on the way."

"To the banana stand," cried Willow. She whacked Lucy on the back of the thigh with her blue fluffsicle and galloped ahead.

They wandered through the sea of stalls, banners and people wearing shorts in ten-degree weather, as is the Sticky Pines way. It seemed that everybody in the Big Crater Valley was there, losing the rigged games, screaming on the rickety rides and, most of all, eating.

Tex inhaled the scent of freshly fried food as they passed a pink and white striped "Nurro

Churro" cart. "Ah, civilisation," he exhaled. "Mass-produced goodness, and in Sticky Pines, no less. Will wonders never cease?"

"Truly, it's a miracle," Lucy groused.

"Do not tell me," said Tex. "You believe there is some sort of conspiracy among the concession stands? Are all the rides run by lizard people?"

"It's simpler than that," said Lucy. "I don't trust Fisher."

"Do not say that to Milo," said Tex.

"I think he knows," sighed Lucy.

They headed towards the centre of the fairground, where The Sticky Six were playing "Walk of Life". A sizable gathering of festival-goers sat on blankets and deck chairs around the central stage.

Three sets of paramedics in Nu Co.-branded coveralls looked out over the crowd from the top of the knoll. *There's medical tents and paramedics everywhere. That's weird, isn't it?*

The band finished the song as the kids snaked their way through the crowd. Willow hollered to get her dad's attention, jumping up and down and waving her hands.

Silas spotted them and winked. He whispered something to Janet, the denim-clad bass player. She strummed a riff on her electric instrument: *binka dinka binka dinka binka dinka binka dinka binka dinka binka dinka.* Then Silas and Scruffy Steve started in with the guitar and drums: *Dah! Dah, Duh Dah! Dah, Duh Dah! Dah Dah Doww!* Bernard, the slender singer, wailed out the first line as all four members of The Sticky Six joined in a rousing rendition of "Eye of the Tiger".

Willow cheered and Tex wiggled in a way that resembled dancing. Even Lucy couldn't resist the urge to bop her head.

A group of teenage girls rocked out to the music, obliviously sloshing red Nushie Slushies on Lucy's shoes. They teetered towards the stage in high heels, a paramedic following closely behind as if worried they would break their ankles.

Silas held the final note and shook the neck of his guitar dramatically.

"Woohoooo!" cried Willow and Lucy.

A clown with a pink Afro, red nose and rainbow-striped braces appeared and whispered something to Bernard.

The lead singer nodded. "And now," he crooned, dabbing sweat from his brow, "a word from our sponsor."

Silas blew a kiss to his daughters and disappeared with the other band members behind the red curtain at the back of the stage.

Smoke billowed on to the platform and an epic swell of generic heavy metal music blasted from the speakers.

Lucy covered her ears. *Frickity frack, that's loud.*

The fake fog parted, revealing Carlos Felina, dashing Sticky Pines weatherman, standing at centre stage in a lavender suit and tie. "Greetings, Sticky Pines," he said into the microphone. "How is everybody feeling today?"

The audience whooped and hollered. Tex stuck two fingers in his mouth and whistled shrilly, nearly splitting Lucy's eardrums.

"Welcome to The First Annual Nu Co. Par-T in Da Pines!" Carlos exclaimed, his too-white teeth glinting under his pencil-thin moustache. "Please join me in thanking the good people of Nu Co. for their hard work in putting together the best carnival this town has ever seen!"

Lucy tried not to gag as the crowd ate it up; just like they were eating up everything Nu Co. was dishing out that day. She had never seen so many people eat so much food. The bins were overflowing with clown-adorned wrappers, bags and empty cups.

"As the oldest business in the Big Crater Valley," said Carlos, "Sticky Sweet has been manufactured in Sticky Pines for over a hundred years."

A man in cowboy boots two rows down whooped loudly.

"And now," Carlos continued with a wink,

"with this brand-new concentrated formula, our sappy little product could soon become the biggest little sweetener in the country."

"Eat it, honey!" yelled a middle-aged bald man Lucy recognised with alarm as the town dentist.

"And none of this would have been possible," Carlos paused for dramatic effect, "without Nu Co.'s CEO, Mr Richard Fisher!"

Please, no.

The music played again and the man himself stepped out from behind the red curtain. Confetti cannons fired over the audience, the members of which "oohed" and "aahed". Mr Fisher shook Carlos's hand.

"Thank you all for such a warm welcome." Fisher's deep voice reverberated over the crowd. "I hope everyone is having a good time."

An enthusiastic red-headed woman near the kids applauded so loudly she looked like she was having a seizure. Lucy had seen her before, at the candle store downtown that always smelled like burning sage. She usually seemed much more serene. Two paramedics nearly knocked Lucy over as they ran up and grabbed the woman by the shoulders.

What the bunk?

"Get your hands off me," the woman shouted. "What do you think you're doing?" Then her hands started to shake.

"Get her to the tent," the female paramedic barked to the male one. They grabbed the struggling woman around the waist and hurried her away from the throng.

What the hangnail was that? Lucy felt queasy as she watched them go, and not just because she hadn't eaten since breakfast.

"I think everyone is enjoying themselves," Carlos laughed. "Maybe a little too much." He elbowed Mr Fisher playfully in the side.

Mr Fisher chuckled. "Sticky Pines is a unique little town," he said, "and in the short time we've been here, we've learned just how special it is. This carnival is our way of saying thank you, from the bottom of our hearts." He waved to the crowd, to thunderous applause.

Lucy scowled. *I have no time for this donked-up applesauce.*

Mr Fisher bared his teeth in a reptilian grin. "Be sure to try all of our products," he added. "Now with Nucralose!"

A series of goofy clowns trotted into the audience, dispersing all variety of Nu Co. food and drink.

A woman in tight-fitting coveralls, with big blonde hair and eyelashes that could be seen from space, entered the stage. She presented Carlos with an oversized wad of pink NuCotton Candy. The suave local celebrity stuffed a large wad in his mouth.

"We're leaving now," Lucy hissed at Tex, who was downing his third free sample of Nu Co. Cola.

Mr Fisher winked and waved at the frenzied congregation as the clowns danced around idiotically, handing out an endless supply of goodies. Fisher locked eyes with Lucy and his smile faded.

She didn't know what Fisher was up to, but she knew one thing for sure: nothing good ever came with this many clowns.

CHAPTER 9

Banana Drama

A pair of clowns in oversized polka-dot trousers traipsed past Lucy, Tex and Willow as they made their way to the banana stand.

"There's something off about this carnival," said Lucy.

"Relax, Lucinski." Tex pulled out the anthropomorphic strawberry and juggled it from one hand to the other. "This carnival is a friendly gesture. Do not look a gift horse in the mouth."

"Tell that to the Trojans," Lucy muttered.

They reached the frozen banana stand: a metal structure shaped like the bottom half of a banana sticking out of the ground. It was situated at the end of the row across from the mechanical bull, slightly off-centre, as if it had been constructed at the last minute. Intriguingly, the yellow hut was adorned with signs proclaiming "Nucralose Free!" and "Nutritious and Delicious!"

Huh. That's refreshing.

The kids waited in line as the proprietor, a man dressed as the top half of a banana, served customers. His face was painted yellow with black spots to match the rest of his costume.

"Welcome to the banana stand. I am the banana man," he said when they reached the front of the line. "How may I fix your banana?"

"You got any nuts?" asked Willow.

"Walnuts or peanuts, crushed, crumbled or sliced. All my bananas are dipped in the most delectable chocolate you've ever tasted. Just don't ask for any Nucralose," he added with a sneer. "That stuff is nothing but trouble."

"Fine by me," said Lucy. She was thrilled to

find somebody else who shared her prejudice, even if it was a somebody dressed like a piece of fruit. "I'll take one with walnuts, please."

"Same for me," said Willow.

"I will take peanuts, actually," said Tex. "I appreciate the eternal struggle between salty and sweet."

The man dipped the first banana carefully and swirled it, once, twice, three times, before rolling it in a tray of crushed walnuts and handing it to Willow. He wiped his brow with the back of his plastic-gloved hand, smearing the paint that obscured his features.

"Hey, look." Willow held her sunglasses-sporting toy strawberry up in front of the costumed man. "You're both fruit people. Can we get a picture?"

"No pictures," snapped the banana man. Without another word, he haphazardly dunked two bananas in chocolate, handed them to Willow and slammed the shutters.

"But I wanted peanuts," Tex groused. He took

his treat, the messy chocolate dribbling down his fingers.

Willow knocked on the stand. "Sorry, Mr Banana, I didn't mean to upset you."

There was no response from within. Willow shrugged. She waved a frozen banana in front of her sister's face, but Lucy's attention was elsewhere.

Strolling down the bustling row of vendors was Milo Fisher, looking quite different from usual. He was wearing a blue-sleeved baseball shirt tucked into a pair of jeans, and a matching blue baseball cap.

Whoa. He almost looks normal.

He walked with his head down, as if he was trying not to be noticed, which, naturally, produced the opposite effect.

"Hey, Feesh!" Tex shouted and waved.

Milo looked startled as he spotted Lucy's group. He looked around furtively and picked his way towards them through the crowd.

"Howdy, stranger," Tex saluted.

"Hey," Milo responded. He smiled flatly at the Sladan sisters. "Hi."

"Hi," said Willow.

Lucy waved and took a bite of her banana. It was mouth-wateringly delicious. It had a bit of an earthy kick, like Mexican hot chocolate.

"Is that a NuCo. product?" asked Milo, peering at her sloppy-looking treat. He glanced warily at the "Nucralose Free!" sign on the yellow stand. "This place doesn't look very professional."

"Tastes fine to me," said Lucy.

"How have you been?" Tex clapped Milo on the back. "We have not seen you in ages."

"I'm fantastic," said Milo unconvincingly. He turned to Lucy. "How about you?"

"Never better."

"Nuh-uh," Willow scoffed. "You've been sulking in your room listening to recordings of animal howls and drawing scary pictures of Bigwoof."

Lucy felt heat rush to her face.

Tex nudged Willow. "Uh, Weeloski, I think it

is time for you to win some more prizes, yeah?"

"I do need to finish my mission," Willow agreed. "I'm gonna win at all the games at this fair," she explained to Milo.

"Ambitious," he nodded.

"Any tips on how to beat them?" said Lucy. "This is your dad's carnival, after all."

"Not a one," said Milo. "I've never been to a carnival like this before. It's been ... interesting."

Just then, the shutters to the stand flew clamorously open. Lucy and Milo each jumped a foot in the air.

The banana man stood in the open hut window, a smile on his paint-striped face. "Oh. Did I scare you? My apologies." He turned to Milo. Would you like a nutritious frozen treat, young man?"

"Oh, uh, sure," said Milo. He pulled out a black-leather wallet and fished out a twenty.

Willow pulled on Lucy's arm. "C'mon, let's do more games."

Lucy caught Tex's eye. "You guys go ahead.

I'll catch up with you later."

"That is a fantastic plan, Lucille." Tex put his arm around Willow and led her back towards the crowd. "Take your time," he called over his shoulder.

Willow made a kissy face at Lucy as the pair trotted off.

They were alone, at last. Except for the banana man, who was busily twirling his latest confection.

Lucy leaned against the stand. "So," she said.

"So," Milo replied.

"So," said the big yellow man, rolling a banana in the tray of walnuts. "You kids have such interesting conversations these days. What exactly is a 'big woof'?"

"You were eavesdropping?" said Milo. "That's rude."

"Is it?" said the man. "You were speaking in front of my stand. I merely happened to be within."

Lucy was more than happy to talk about

something important, for once. "Bigwoof is a massive hairy monster that's been lurking in the woods around Sticky Pines." She leaned in and lowered her voice. "I think it might be responsible for the missing people around here. Not that anybody cares."

"You do realise that you sound crazy," said Milo.

"At least the banana guy is interested in hearing about it," said Lucy. "Anyway, it doesn't matter who I tell. Nobody believes me."

"Because this whole Bigwoof thing is totally ridiculous," said Milo.

"A big hairy monster," the man said thoughtfully. He set the banana in the cooling tray. "How intriguing. And what are your names, if I may ask?"

"Lucy Sladan," said Lucy. "And this is Milo Fisher."

"Don't tell people my full name," said Milo.

"Why not?" said Lucy.

Milo glowered at her. "Because I said so."

"It's a pleasure to meet you both," said the man. He held out Milo's artfully crafted frozen treat. As Milo reached up to take it, the man grabbed him by the wrist and pulled him up to the window of the hut.

"What are you doing?" Milo shouted. "Let go of me."

"So," hissed the man. "You're Fisher's boy." He pinched Milo's chin with his black-gloved hand and examined his face.

"What the heck?" Lucy grabbed Milo around the waist and pulled.

"Ouch! Stop!" Milo screamed.

Lucy wasn't sure if he was talking to her or the banana, but she did not loosen her grip.

"Do you know what your father has done?" the banana man snarled, squeezing Milo's wrist. "Do you know where he took them?"

"I don't know what you're talking about!" Milo bit the man's fingers as hard as he could.

"Owww!" yelped the man. He released his grip.

Milo and Lucy tumbled to the ground and scrambled out of reach.

"What's going on here?" boomed a voice behind them.

The banana man squeaked and disappeared inside his stand, slamming the shutters tight.

Milo helped Lucy to her feet, each checking that the other was intact. Shaking but otherwise unscathed, they turned around to thank their rescuer.

Lucy's breath caught in her throat. Before them was a hideous big-footed creature.

She had never been so happy to see a clown in her life.

CHAPTER 10

Clowns

"Are you injured?" asked the clown, his voice flat and authoritative.

Milo and Lucy dusted themselves off and took stock of their rescuer. He was tall and hefty, the improbable size of his red shoes and curly orange wig making him seem even larger. A wide blue smile had been drawn over his white-painted face, and, like all the other clowns at the festival, he wore an oblong red nose. His orange-striped clothes were complete with fingerless gloves and a flower on his lapel that Lucy suspected squirted water. On any other day she would have run away screaming, but at this moment she couldn't help but feel grudgingly grateful.

Maybe they're not terrible masked monsters after all, but costumed crusaders? "I think we're OK," she said, heart still pounding.

"What happened?" asked the clown.

"That guy just attacked us for no reason." Lucy's panic drained away, leaving anger in its wake. She turned to Milo, who was rubbing his wrist and looking more shaken than when he was almost mauled by a bear. "What the chudmuffin was that about?"

"I don't know," said Milo. "What is this stand even doing here? Nu Co. doesn't sell frozen bananas."

"That's affirmative," the clown responded. He frowned at the "Nucralose Free!" sign posted on the side of the shack. "I suspect this is an unauthorised food stand." He swept his arm out authoritatively. "Step aside, please."

Lucy and Milo backed into the thoroughfare of oblivious festival-goers. A group of revellers scarfing FunNu Cakes and Nurro Churros paused to stare at the commotion.

The clown banged on the stand. "Open up," he demanded.

There was no response. He tried to prise open the shutters with his fingers, but they wouldn't budge.

The clown knocked again. "Open up and identify yourself!"

Again, no answer. The clown stuck two fingers in his mouth and whistled. Two more clowns, one slender and one squat, pushed through the crowd. These bozos were dressed identically in blue pageboy wigs, green striped shirts and red braces.

Tweedle Dum and Tweedle Dummer.

The Dums stood at attention by the banana stand and saluted.

"Looks like we've got a rogue agent here, gentlemen," the orange clown bellowed. "Prepare to infiltrate."

"Infiltrate?" Lucy whispered. "Is he the captain of some sort of clown army?"

The slender one (*Mr Dum*) reached into his baggy blue trousers and pulled out a crowbar.

What the—

Mr Dum inserted the crowbar between the shutters and, operating as one, the costumed men yanked with great force until the doors flew open with a deafening CRONCH!

The Captain hoisted himself through the window while the Dums stood side by side, blocking any avenue of escape, and any view of what was going on inside.

Lucy heard pots and pans being tossed about, followed by a metallic crash and an oozy splash that she realised, regretfully, was the pot of delicious melted chocolate. After a few moments, the Dums parted and the Clown Captain clambered grouchily through the window, his oversized trousers smeared with chocolate. "There's nobody in there."

The curious crowd dispersed. Lucy stood on tiptoe and peered inside the empty stand. It was true. The banana man was nowhere to be seen.

"Where did he go?" said Milo. Lucy had never seen him look so angry. "Don't tell me, was he taken by unicorns?" he sneered. "Abducted by gnomes? Maybe he turned invisible."

"What's your problem?" said Lucy.

"Weird stuff always seems to happen when you're around."

"How is any of this *my* fault?" said Lucy, her blood boiling. "This is your dad's carnival."

"Oh, so now this is *his* fault?" said Milo.

"I wouldn't put anything past him. He messed with the picture of Bigwoof and you know it."

"Oh, everything's always about your big dumb hairy monster," Milo fumed. "Don't you have anything better to do than obsess about creatures that don't exist?"

"I obsess about plenty." She poked Milo's chest. "For instance, why is your dad the world's biggest blowhole?"

"He's not a blowhole," Milo snapped. "Maybe you're the blowhole."

"Oh yeah?" Lucy huffed. "Well, maybe you're a—"

"What did you kids say about a big hairy monster?" the Clown Captain cut in.

Milo and Lucy looked around to see that all three clowns were standing stock-still, staring at them. Aside from their painted-on grins, the men's faces were expressionless.

The Captain placed a finger on his wig-obscured ear and spoke into his flower. "Sir? We may have a problem here."

"Who is he talking to?" whispered Lucy.

"I don't know," Milo whispered back, "but I'm really starting to hate this banana stand."

Two more clowns approached, one with curly red hair and the other with purple hair like Lucy's. They stood imposingly at either side of the kids.

Lucy's fear of clowns had now returned in full force. "Is it just me, or does it seem like they're not here to make balloon animals?"

"For once, you might be right." Milo rubbed

the back of his neck. "My, uh, my dad did mention that he hired a professional security force for the festival."

"Your dad's security forces are dressed as clowns?"

"He didn't want to scare anybody," said Milo.

"Good thinking." Lucy's nostrils flared.

"Two children," said the Captain. He waited for a response. "Yes, sir. They seem to know something about the…" He glanced at Milo and Lucy before walking to the other side of the banana stand, where he spoke too quietly for them to hear.

The other four clowns arranged themselves in a circle around the kids.

"Say something," Lucy urged Milo. "Tell them who you are and make them back off."

"Here's the thing…" Milo looked at his shoes. "I'm not supposed to be here."

"What?"

"My dad made me promise not to come. 'The consequences will be dire'," he said, imitating

Fisher's deep voice.

Lucy was dumbfounded. "Your dad told you not to come to his own carnival? Why?"

Milo frowned. "Good question."

One by one, the clowns pressed their red noses, emitting slurred honking noises like languorous rubber chickens. The plastic noses lit up, illuminating the clowns' faces in eerie red light, blinking slowly, out of sync.

Holy flippin' mother of creamed corn.

"I say we run on the count of three," said Milo. "One…"

"You kids are going to have to come with us," ordered the Captain. He marched towards them as the other clowns advanced in concert.

"Two, three, go!" Lucy yelped.

They ducked through the arms of the red-haired clown. Lucy squealed as Milo yanked her around the banana stand, dodging Mr Dummer and scrambling into the crowd.

"Get back here!" called the Captain, too late.

The kids elbowed their way through the mob

surrounding the mechanical bull and stumbled out the other side.

They turned into a narrow space between a row of tents, tripping on electrical cords and empty paper cups. Milo lifted the back flap of a blue-striped tent and checked for clowns. Satisfied, they slipped through into a cluttered souvenir stall that reeked of incense. For the time being, the coast was clear.

"Why are they chasing us?" asked Lucy, out of breath.

"We'll find out later. First things first." Milo grabbed an orange and blue Nu Co. jester hat from a rack.

"I'm not wearing that," she said.

"It's a disguise." He waved his hands over his torso. "Like I'm wearing."

"That's a disguise?" said Lucy.

"Obviously."

That explains the normal clothes. "You really are hiding from your dad, aren't you?"

"Don't look so smug." He shoved the hideous

hat into her hands. "Now, hurry up and put it on."

Milo handed some money to the dreadlocked lady behind the counter.

"What about you?" asked Lucy.

Milo threw his cap behind a rack of ribbon dancers, then stripped off his baseball shirt and tossed it at Lucy.

"What are you doing?" she asked.

The carnival worker looked up from her fantasy book, glanced at a sign above the counter that said "No Shoes, No Shirt, No Problem!" and went back to reading.

"Give me yours," said Milo.

"Are you nuts?" She pulled at the hem of her wolf T-shirt. "This is my favourite top."

"Just do it."

Lucy muttered under her breath and went back into the alley to change. Milo's shirt smelled like boy's deodorant. She shoved her thick violet hair under the ridiculous jester hat and pulled it low. When she re-entered the tent, she turned her wolf shirt inside out to hide the design, and tossed it to Milo.

He slipped it on and started to tuck it in but Lucy slapped his hands.

"Nobody tucks in Sticky Pines," she said.

"Fine." He grimaced. "How do I look?"

"Mmmm… Hold still." She dug her fingers into his perfectly gelled hair until it stuck out in all directions. "Do you have any scissors?" she asked the lady at the cash register.

The woman rummaged around and handed Lucy a large, pointy pair.

"Whoa, whoa!" Milo waved his hands.

"Relax," said Lucy. She spun him around and cut the label off the shirt, then bent down and cut his jeans at the knee to make shorts. There was nothing to be done about his loafers, but at least his socks were white. "There." She gave him a once-over and nodded her approval.

They edged to the front of the stand and peeked into the crowd. To the right, there were two clowns, one with red hair and one with pink, marching down the thoroughfare, away from them. *At least Fisher's goons are easy to spot.* To the left was the Ferris wheel. The area was filled with snacking townspeople, but it was mercifully clown-free.

Lucy stuck her glasses in her back pocket. The world was blurry, but she could see things up close. "Let's go." She pointed to the wheel, which was about thirty metres away. "We can talk up there."

Milo checked the path and then nodded his approval.

Lucy took a deep breath, stepped out into the aisle and ran straight into the pot belly of a pear-shaped man with a grey ponytail. He was sipping from an extra-large cup of Nu Co. Cola.

This is why glasses are helpful.

She squinted up at the man.

"Scruffy Steve," she exclaimed.

Steve Kozlowski was the drummer of The Sticky Six. He was known for dressing up as

Santa at the Winter Village outside Mandy's Candies.

"Lucy Goosie," he said. "Nice hat, kiddo, I hardly recognised you without the hair." He raised his hand for a high five.

Lucy slapped his palm. "How's it going?" she asked, immediately regretting the question. Steve was a nice guy, but he had a tendency to ramble.

"Oh, you know how it is," said Steve. "My dog Marty had a bad case of eczema, I'm sure ya heard. Well, I got that under control, but now he's suffering from headaches. I was just sayin' to your dad, I feel like I'm comin' down with a headache myself today, must be all the food, but I can't stop eatin' it, it's too good—"

"Aw, man," Lucy cut him off as politely as she could. Milo dug his nails into her wrist. "Eczema, headaches. Hoo boy. Hope you and Marty feel better, Steve. Well, we gotta run."

"Yeah, yeah. Good seeing ya, kid," said Steve. "Hey, by the by, your dad is out looking for you.

And your sister. Where is the little con artist anyway?"

"Uh…" Lucy began.

Milo held out his hand. "Hi, I'm Milo. Pleasure to meet you."

Steve took Milo's hand and slowly grasped the concept of a handshake. "Pleasure's all mine, kid."

"Indeed," said Milo, trying to end the overlong shake.

"Sorry, bro." Steve chuckled and let go. He held up his calloused hands. "Drummer's hooves. Hey, Goose." He turned to Lucy. "Did you get a load of those clowns? What's the deal with the blinking noses? It was funny at first, but now it's starting to bum me out."

Lucy turned and saw a half-dozen costumed commandos marching across the lane towards the bumper cars. "Did they spot us?" she asked Milo.

"I'm not sticking around to find out." He dropped her hand and took off briskly towards the Ferris wheel.

Crudberries. "Sorry, Steve, gotta go."

"Busy busy, just like your dad these days," he chuckled.

"Later," Lucy called over her shoulder.

She caught up with Milo and pulled on his sleeve. "Slow down," she said. "We look suspicious."

He obliged, and they strolled as casually as they could towards their destination. For the moment, their disguises seemed to be working. They were passing the zillionth NuCotton Candy vendor when Mr Dum marched towards them, his red nose flashing brightly.

Lucy felt a purple lock of hair free itself and fall in front of her nose. Horrified, she scrambled to tuck it under the jester hat.

The lanky clown glanced at them out of the corner of his eye, but continued past. As soon as he was a few paces behind them, Lucy breathed a sigh of relief.

Then she glanced back. Mr Dum had stopped

a few metres away. He was speaking into the flower on his lapel.

Lucy tried to pull Milo along faster, but their path was abruptly cut off as the half-dozen clowns they had spotted earlier entered the thoroughfare. They were trapped.

Just then, a plastic garbage can flew high over their heads. It landed with a hollow thud and spilled its contents at the feet of the clowns. The man who threw it stood triumphantly in a nearby intersection. He was dressed as a banana.

"Take that, Zebo," the banana man yelled, fist extended in the air.

The Clown Captain looked down at the garbage.

"It's him," barked a green-haired clown.

The banana man squeaked in alarm, turned tail and took off.

"Primary target is in sight," said the Captian to the oversized daisy on his shirt.

With that, the prismatic posse took off in hot pursuit, leaving Milo and Lucy standing in the middle of the walkway, clasped hands shaking, neither understanding a single thing that had happened in the last twenty minutes.

CHAPTER 11

Going Around
in Circles

"What. The. Bunk," Lucy fumed, repeating the phrase for the umpteenth time.

"Yeah, you said that," said Milo.

They had finally snaked their way to the front of the line in the shadow of the towering Ferris wheel.

"And who is the banana man?" Lucy hissed. "What does he want?"

"You know as much as I do," said Milo.

The pimple-faced teenager running the rickety contraption helped them into their car. He shut the flimsy door and pulled a lever, sending them slowly skyward in the teetering trolley.

Lucy slipped her glasses back on. Now that she could see him in detail, Milo looked more worried than he had let on. "How come your dad doesn't want you at this carnival?" she asked.

"I don't know," he said. "That's why I'm here."

The wheel jerked to a stop to let other people on and off the ride. Milo clutched the central pole to right himself.

"You came because you weren't supposed to?"

"I suppose you're rubbing off on me."

Lucy frowned in approval. "You could do worse."

The wheel started and stopped, their cabin gradually hiccuping past the tree line. They could see most of the carnival now; a sea of games, rides and fluttering colour. But there was something else decorating the landscape: clusters of sinister red lights from security clowns out on patrol.

Are they looking for the banana man, or us?

Milo stuck his fingers through the chain-link panel and peered wistfully over the sunny horizon. "It's funny," he said. "I was really starting to like this place."

"What are you talking about?" asked Lucy.

"I'm leaving." He slumped in his seat. "Or rather, I'm being sent away."

"Sent away?" She steadied herself against the incessant rocking of the Ferris wheel car. "Sent where?"

"My dad's sending me to Kansas."

"To boarding school?" Lucy braced herself against the mesh. "I thought places like that were just a myth to scare kids into behaving."

"Boarding school or Kansas?"

"Both."

Milo laughed ruefully. "Of course you did."

They stopped at the top of the wheel, their pink cabin swaying in the autumn breeze. Now they could see for miles, the mottled autumn canopy of green, amber and indigo extending to the jagged rim of the Dentalia Mountains.

"I thought your dad took you with him everywhere?" Lucy couldn't imagine being sent away from her family.

"He always has," said Milo, exasperated. "This is all my fault. I never should have asked him about that stupid Bigwoof picture." His head fell into his hands.

The wheel started up again. "You asked him?" said Lucy, incredulous. "What did you say? What did he say?"

"He denied that it was Shooped. I told him I didn't believe him. We had a fight." Milo looked like he might cry. "I've never seen him so upset. He said I don't understand how the world works."

"Nobody understands how the world works," said Lucy. "Not really."

Milo stared sullenly at the crowd below.

"When are you leaving?" asked Lucy.

"Monday."

The Ferris wheel picked up speed as they careened past the ground.

"Monday?" She held on to her ridiculous hat. "As in, two days from now?"

"Correct."

"What the sludge?"

"What the sludge, indeed." He smiled faintly. "Guess I'd better make the most of my last weekend of freedom."

Lucy spotted something in the crowd below that made her duck to the bottom of the car, coughing on her own spit.

"What?" whispered Milo anxiously. "Did the clowns see us?"

"Get down," Lucy hissed.

She pulled him behind the plastic door, causing the car to tilt. He awkwardly peeked through the mesh as they sped past the crowd, where a man in a lavender suit was signing autographs for a group of giggling girls.

"Who's that?" he asked.

"Carlos Felina. The weatherman."

Carlos stepped out of line and began talking to an orange-clad clown.

"Oh, for the love of Björk," Lucy groaned. "Now he's talking to the Clown Captain."

"Why are we hiding from him? Does he even know who you are?"

"I don't think so." Lucy scratched her sweaty scalp. "Normally I would consider him the most trusted newsman in Sticky Pines, but today he's with *them*."

"*Them?*" said Milo. He ripped a stray thread off the bottom of his new shorts and tossed it to the grimy floor. "You mean my dad."

Lucy pushed her glasses up her nose. "Well, I mean…"

He looked up. "What? Say what you're thinking."

If Lucy was going to tell Milo about her suspicions, it was now or never. She gripped the centre pole tightly. "I think your dad's hiding something. Something big. Why did he Shoop the photo? Why didn't he want you to come here? Why all the security clowns? Fish, he's trying to keep you away from something he doesn't want you to see."

"You don't know that." Milo startled Lucy with a finger in her face. "My father hasn't done anything wrong, not to you or anyone else."

"Other than covering up the greatest supernatural evidence the world has ever seen?"

"Ugh, every time I think you and I can be friends you say something like that. Listen to yourself. You sound *ridiculous*."

"Do I?" said Lucy. "DO I?" she asked loudly enough that Milo covered her mouth with his hand. She squirmed but he didn't let go, so she licked his palm.

"Come on," he said, recoiling and wiping his hand on his freshly cut shorts.

Lucy poked his shoulder. "Your dad *lied to you*."

He poked her back. "So what if he did? Maybe he had a good reason."

"That's baloney and you know it," she scoffed.

Milo turned away as the Ferris wheel jolted to a stop at the very top.

Lucy couldn't remember the last time she'd seen such a beautiful day in Sticky Pines. The sky remained cloudless, as if it had been tidied up just for the occasion. A sparrow darted by, chirped a complaint and disappeared over the forest. She noticed a hazy splotch in the distance, past the abyss of Black Hole Lake. The wheel started up again, gaining speed for one last turn around the circle.

"Why is there smoke coming from the factory?"

"Because it's a factory?" Milo responded.

"But everyone who works there is here."

"Everything is an unsolvable mystery to you, isn't it?" said Milo. As they passed the base of the Ferris wheel, he spotted something disturbing. "Uh, Lucy?" He pointed at a commotion down below. "I think there's something wrong with the weatherman."

A crowd had gathered below. The Clown Captain was speaking urgently into his flower. Lying on the ground in the midst of it all was

Carlos Felina, twisting and writhing like a man possessed by demons.

Lucy gasped as they flew by the horrific scene. A murmur radiated around the wheel as other passengers registered the commotion.

"What's wrong with him?" asked Milo.

A woman in a white coat hustled over, followed by four paramedics with a stretcher. She injected something into the twitching man.

Carlos's convulsions stopped. The paramedics hoisted him on to the pallet. The clowns cleared a path and whisked the weatherman into a nearby medical tent.

The wheel jerked towards the ground. Their ride was nearly over.

"We need to follow them," said Lucy. "All the weird stuff is connected, Fish. Bigwoof, boarding school, the bozos… Even the banana man." Lucy's mind raced. "I know it is."

"Or maybe you're just seeing things that aren't there." Milo slid out of his seat as their car lurched again.

"We're so close to finding the truth."

"Some people say there's no such thing as truth."

"Yeah, those people are called 'liars'," said Lucy.

Milo stared at the floor as if trying to divine from the leftover candy wrappers and dusky smears of chewing gum the answer to some cryptic, unanswerable question. "All right. I'm in."

"You are?" asked Lucy, surprised. Gleefully, she cemented their renewed partnership with a handshake.

Their car reached the ground and the pimple-faced technician opened the gate to let them off. The kids stepped out, knees wobbling. They milled through the exit, keeping an eye out for clowns or other signs of impending doom.

"Lucy," Milo whispered.

"Yeah?" she whispered back.

"What if you don't like it?"

"What?"

"The truth," he said.

Lucy considered this. "I'll tell you what I don't like," she said. "I don't like how much of the world seems to run on lies."

Milo was about to speak, but Lucy anticipated the question and cut him off.

"And once I know what's going on, I'll shout it from the treetops, because the Truth is the only thing that matters in this tricked-out, photoshopped world."

"One thing's for sure." Milo fluffed his uncombed hair. "You're not boring."

"That's been scientifically verified," said Lucy. She looked at him expectantly. "What are we waiting for?"

"I'm following you."

"Oh," she said. "Right." She turned on her heel. "This way."

The duo crossed the crowded expanse, single file, like ducklings seeking shelter in a storm. Not far in the mountainous distance, dark clouds encroached on the horizon.

CHAPTER 12

Monstrous Medicine

Lucy and Milo slipped between a green Nu Co. Cola tent and a glittery corn dog stand with a sign that read "Now Serving Nu Co. Ketchup!" Sidestepping the cords and detritus that littered their path, they made their way down a shadowy alley between the vendors. At last, they reached the back of the medical tent where Carlos Felina had been taken.

Lucy peeked through a gap in the white vinyl while Milo stood on tiptoe to see inside. The small structure was packed with clowns and medical personnel. The weatherman squirmed on a bed on wheels in the centre, wailing like a wild animal.

The sedating substance he had been injected with seemed to have worn off. It took four fully grown clowns to hold down his slight, spasming body. One of Carlos's hands jutted out, his splayed fingers swollen and sweating, the skin on his knuckles cracked and peeling.

Holy stickball. What's happening to him?

Milo recoiled in horror, but Lucy couldn't look away. She held her breath, hardly daring to blink.

The woman in the white coat and cat-eye glasses pulled the Captain aside, towards the corner where the kids were spying.

"His condition is accelerating," she said. "We need to take him to the lab as soon as possible." She jotted some notes furiously on her clipboard.

"This guy's a mess, doc," said the Captain. He was still covered in chocolate from the banana stand. "How much of the stuff has he eaten?"

"Enough," said the doctor. "We're still trying

to establish the threshold."

Amid the chaos around the bed, Lucy heard a wet *thwepping* sound. What had initially looked like sweat was now dripping off Carlos like egg whites. Lucy gagged. Milo looked green.

The Captain recoiled. "What's that stuff coming off him?"

"Slime," said a familiar deep voice.

Mr Fisher. Lucy pinched Milo's arm. He swatted her hand away before she could draw blood.

"Slime?" the Captain snorted.

"It's not a scientific term, Mr Murl." Fisher waltzed into view at the back of the teeming tent. "The discharge seems to be a by-product of this –" he waved his hand, outlining Carlos's body in the air – "process."

The doctor nodded. "His anatomy is beginning to morph. Terminal and vellus filaments will sprout on the extremities first, before spreading over the rest of the epidermis." She underlined something on her clipboard.

"English, please?" said the Captain.

"He'll grow hair all over his body," said Fisher.

Lucy covered her mouth to keep from crying out.

"How many more people are like this?" asked the Captain.

"Just two, from today," said the doctor. She furrowed her brow. "Fewer than expected. A disappointing result."

Disappointing? Is this ratchet brain saying they want this to happen to people?

"Put him in the van," said Fisher, referring to the weatherman. "Take him to the factory with the others."

"With all due respect, Sir, we don't need another vehicle torn to shreds," groused a buck-toothed clown. His yellow wig was the shape of a haystack. "That teacher creature we picked up the other day was more trouble than she was worth."

Teacher creature? Lucy felt like her brain was

about to explode. *Could he be talking about Mrs Stricks?*

"Strap him down," Fisher ordered. "Tightly." He stepped aside, towards the gap through which Lucy and his son were watching, so close they could smell his spicy aftershave. "We take no chances this time, understood?"

"Yes, sir," saluted the Captain. "You heard the man," he barked to the rest of the tent.

Lucy stood slack-jawed as the paramedics covered Carlos with a thin silver blanket and wheeled him out of the tent. Fisher, the Captain and the doctor followed closely behind. A scattering of clowns was left to clean up the slimy mess.

A moment later they heard an engine start, followed by the sound of a large vehicle making its way to the periphery of the fairground.

Lucy staggered back, a bazillion thoughts colliding in her head.

Milo leaned queasily against the tent. Lucy grabbed his arm and led him down the alley to an area buzzing with the sound of electrical generators. The air smelled like exhaust, but the noise made it unlikely they would be overheard.

"What did I just see?" said Milo. "That slime… Ugh, it was revolting."

"Forget the slime," said Lucy. "Don't you see what's happening?"

"What do you mean?"

"It's the food!" she cried over the din. "Nucralose. Your dad's new version, at least."

"Nucralose?"

"Didn't you hear the doctor? Eating Nu Co. food did something to Carlos Felina. They said he's gonna grow hair. Everywhere." Lucy chewed off the corner of her thumbnail and spat it on the grass.

"But it's just a sweetener made of tree sap," said Milo.

"It used to be, but it's not any more," said Lucy. "Now it's something else."

"Maybe he's allergic?"

Lucy waved wildly at the medical tent. "Did

that look like an allergic reaction to you?"

Milo shook his head dizzily. "I don't know. I don't have any allergies."

"The footprint changed," Lucy went on, circling him. "The casts in my room. The foot changed. You saw it. And the slime we found at the Strickses' house – like the stuff coming off Carlos – my mom said there was Nucralose in it, remember?" She gasped. "Holy smokes. The Other Mrs Stricks was the Bigwoof that saved us from the bear!"

Milo sat on an upturned crate and put his head in his hands. "Can you please stop jabbering and start speaking sense?"

"Don't you see?" She clasped his hands. "Fish, your dad's sweetener is turning people into monsters."

Milo blinked, incredulous. "You're nuts. You are one hundred per cent in-the-bank bonkers."

"It may sound bitcoin batspit," said Lucy, "but it's true. Everyone at this carnival is in danger. We have to warn them."

"Warn them?"

Lucy shook her head. "No, you're right, it's too late for that. Everyone's been eating this stuff all day." She paced up and down the aisle. "Your dad said they were taking Carlos to the factory. He said there were others there, Fish. *Others*."

"Only about half the words you're saying make any sense."

Lucy snapped her fingers. "That's where the Strickses are. They've been there this whole time. And Alastair Chelon and Mandy Millepoids. They're all at the factory."

"This is crazy," Milo muttered. "You're crazy." He pulled out his smartphone. "I'm calling my dad. He'll clear this whole thing up."

"You can't call him," Lucy fumed. "He's the one who's responsible."

Milo paused with his finger over the call button. "He's my father. He'll tell me what's going on."

"Like he told you the truth about the picture? Come on, Fish, you can't—"

CRASH!

A stack of wooden pallets toppled over behind Lucy. Milo thrust his arm in front of her as something big and yellow stumbled into the corridor.

The kids gaped as the banana man steadied himself, his hands on his knees. He glanced up at them guiltily. Then he turned and sprinted down the narrow aisle.

"Oh no you don't!" Lucy snatched the shiny phone from Milo's hand and chucked it at the banana man's feet.

"What are you doing?" cried Milo.

The phone caught the man in the heel with a THWACK. Top-heavy from the bulky rubber costume, he staggered and fell to the ground. Lucy ran and tackled him from behind.

"What is your deal, freakazoid?" she demanded, pushing down on him with all her weight.

He shook Lucy off easily and rolled over, holding his arms out in a gesture of peace.

"Please," he implored, out of breath. "Don't cry out." He held a finger to his lips and pointed out to the fairground. "*They* will hear you."

Lucy peered down a side alley and glimpsed a shock of green hair as one of Fisher's clowns marched past. She glared back at the banana man, unsure whether he or the clown was more of a threat. Much of his face paint had melted off since she saw him last. Strangely, he looked almost familiar.

Criminy peatmoss. "I know who you are," said Lucy. "You're Mandy Millepoids."

"You are correct, you little brute." Grunting, he clambered artlessly to his feet.

"Mandy Millepoids?" Milo picked up his phone and winced as tiny shards of glass rained down on to the grass.

"The second guy who went missing," Lucy exclaimed. "He owns the candy store downtown."

"The guy who—" Milo seemed to snap out of a daze. "Why did you attack me?" he demanded.

"I'm sorry." Millepoids bowed apologetically. "But you are Fisher's son. You know what is happening here. You know what Nu Co. is doing."

"I told you." Lucy punched Milo in the arm, causing his shattered phone to drop to the ground again. "Oh snap," she said, realising what she'd done to his expensive device. "Sorry." She picked it up and tried to turn it on, with no luck.

Milo snatched it back and tossed it over his shoulder. "What are you doing here?" he barked at the banana man. "You don't work for my father."

"I've come with a cure." Millepoids reached into his costume and pulled out a brown paper packet, like the kind they used at Mandy's Candies. He unfolded it and displayed its contents: about twenty chocolate truffles topped with finely chopped nuts.

"Candy?" said Lucy.

"Medicinal candy," said Millepoids. "I've been working on it for weeks. It prevents the

'Big Woof' transformation, as you call it. Given enough time, it can even reverse it."

"You put this in the chocolate at the banana stand, didn't you?" said Lucy.

Millepoids nodded

"You gave everyone an antidote to Nucralose!" Lucy was awed by his ingenuity.

"Not everyone," said Millepoids. "Only those who enjoy tasty frozen fruit."

Milo scoffed. "You're saying this nonsense about Nucralose is true and taking candy from strangers is the cure?" He threw up his hands. "This whole town is insane."

"Where have you been, Mr Millepoids?" asked Lucy. "The sheriff's been looking for you everywhere."

"I've been hiding from Nu Co., healing myself and helping poor Esther," said Millepoids.

"Esther… That's the Other Mrs Stricks," said Lucy. "You know where she is?"

Millepoids nodded. "She's safe. I found her wandering in the woods, looking … unwell."

His face darkened. "At least I found her before *they* did. I need to find Carlos." He held up the packet of candy. "I can help him."

"You're too late," said Lucy. "They took him to the factory."

"So that's where they've been keeping them," said Millepoids. "They're not safe there. Fisher will dissect them all."

"My father wouldn't hurt anybody," Milo insisted.

"So you say," said Millepoids. "I must get to the factory. Now. Are you going there too?"

"No." Milo kicked a fallen crate. "Absolutely not."

"Good," said Millepoids, backing away slowly. "Do not go to the factory. It's much too dangerous for children." He tossed Lucy the package. "If you see anyone in need, give them one of those. Before it's too late." Without another word, he ran down a side alley and out of sight.

Lucy took a candy out of the package and

sniffed it.

"Don't eat that!" Milo whacked the truffle out of her hand, sending it rolling under a dusty tent flap.

"I already did, at the banana stand," Lucy answered. "Want one?"

Milo sneered.

"Suit yourself." She put the packet into her back pocket, where it stuck out but stayed. "I'm going to the factory. You coming?"

"You can't be serious." Milo stomped on a discarded cup adorned with a clown face, spraying his shins with half-melted blue slush. "Even the crazy banana guy said not to go."

"Please," Lucy snorted. "He was clearly speaking in code." She strode down the long row of vendors.

A stack of soda crates blocked the end of the alleyway. Lucy shoved them to create enough space to squeeze through. Milo stopped her with a hand on her shoulder.

"Wait," he said.

"I'm tired of waiting."

He shoved a few loose grape-coloured locks under her jester hat. "I don't want you to be clown food."

"Oh. Thanks."

They re-entered the carnival and found themselves surrounded by the symphonic chimes of plastic on glass bottles. They were at the ring toss, where Tex and Willow were counting up their prizes.

"Happy horgon, you guys switched clothes?" said Tex, spotting the pair. "That is adorable."

"Tex," said Lucy, relieved.

He was carrying double the number of prizes since they'd seen him last.

"Mom was looking for you," said Willow. "We told her you were in the bathroom with stomach problems."

"Gee, thanks," said Lucy. She scanned the crowd for clowns. "Look, there's no time to explain, but everyone at this carnival is in danger. Everyone who didn't eat a frozen banana, that is."

"What?" Tex laughed.

Lucy took out a handful of medicinal truffles and shoved them into Willow's hip sack. "Give these to our families, and tell them to stop eating anything with Nucralose."

"Stop eating?" Tex blanched. "Now, wait just a minute—"

Lucy turned to Milo. "Are you coming to the factory or not?"

He threw up an arm. "Sure, why not?" he said. "I've lived a long life."

"Let's go." Lucy pulled him towards the back entrance to the carnival.

"You're gonna be grounded till you're forty!" Willow shouted. She turned to Tex. "Come on," she clucked. "It's time to tattle."

CHAPTER 13

Watchers in the Woods

Milo and Lucy legged it out of the carnival through the travelling workers' campsite, past harrumphing generators, hot-dog-scented grills and dirt-caked caravans.

Once in the woods, they followed a meandering stream through a large grove of sticky pines. Lucy scrambled up a lichen-spotted boulder to see how far ahead the lake was.

Milo seemed transfixed by the dark ooze flowing down one of the knurled trunks. "So let me try to understand what you have come to believe."

Lucy stood precariously on tiptoe. "Yes?"

"You're saying that the sap from these trees, right here in front of us, is capable of turning human beings into hideous hairy creatures."

"No." She dropped down to her heels. "I'm saying Nu Co. did something freaky to the sap. That's what makes it turn people into hideous hairy creatures. The trees have been around for gajillions of years and nobody's turned into a Bigwoof before."

Milo pulled a taffy-thick grape-sized glob of sap off the trunk. "This stuff doesn't look like much, does it?" He rolled the substance between his fingers and felt it harden into a squishy bead. When he released the tension, the sap softened and spread over his hand like honey. He sniffed it. "What does it taste like? I mean, before they turn it into sweetener."

"You haven't licked a tree yet?" said Lucy. "That's usually the first thing people do when they get to Sticky Pines."

"I suppose I'm different from the people who traditionally come here."

"Well, you do have all your teeth…"

Milo scrunched his face and licked the sap. "It tastes … piney." He dripped a bit more on to his tongue. "It's sweet, but there's a sort of coppery aftertaste. I don't really get the appeal." He smacked his lips a few times before finding, to his horror, that his tongue was stuck to the roof of his mouth. He squealed like a dying rabbit before prising it loose with a finger.

Lucy laughed so hard she almost fell off the boulder.

Milo spat out the black residue. "Blechh." He wiped his sticky hand on the inside-out shirt he was wearing. "Ith won'th cong oth."

"Yeah." Lucy wiped away a tear. "That stuff won't come off your skin for a day or two." She slid back down to the ground.

Milo scraped his tongue with his teeth. "I'm glad you find this so entertaining. You could have warned me."

"But then I'd be breaking the Sticky Pines tradition." She slapped him on the back.

They tromped briskly alongside the creek, the noise from the carnival dissipating into birdsong, burbling waters and the faint flutter of falling leaves.

"What is *that* disturbing thing?" said Milo, who had spotted something hanging from a low bough on a tall tree. Vaguely human-shaped, it was made of sticks and twine, with a large pine cone for a head.

"It's a birdfeeder," said Lucy. "The birdwatchers coat it with sap and put seeds on it. The birds come to eat, and the watchers watch." She glanced around the area. "There's probably a blind nearby."

"A blind?" asked Milo.

"A little hut where the birdwatchers hide. The good ones are hard to spot."

"So someone could be watching us right now?" said Milo.

"Probably not," said Lucy. "There's no seed on the feeder."

"Birdwatching is kind of a creepy pastime,

isn't it?"

"Sure. From the bird's perspective." Lucy heard a rustle in an alder tree a few paces away. "Hey, look at that."

An owl sat on a high branch. Brown streaks graced its white belly, its curious dark eyes circled by mottled rings of white and grey. It seemed to be staring at them.

"Talk about birdwatching," Milo shuddered. "I thought owls only came out at night."

"Mostly," said Lucy, "but not always. You often see owls out during the day in Sticky Pines."

"Really? That's odd."

"Is it?" She shrugged.

A magpie swooped up and joined the owl on the branch. The black and white bird mirrored the owl's pose, eyeing the children with interest.

"I thought owls ate magpies," said an increasingly perplexed Milo. "This is like one of those videos where a bunny rabbit hangs out with a coyote."

"Kinda like us," said Lucy. "Come on, let's hurry."

They could still hear the distant sounds of rock music from the carnival when they reached the glittering shores of Black Hole Lake. The large body of water was almost perfectly round and very deep, and sat at the centre of the Big Crater Valley. Steam rose steadily from the inky surface in defiance of the crisp autumn air.

"It's rather pretty, for a lake with such a sinister name." Milo approached the water's edge, glassy yellow pebbles crunching under his loafers. "One of the missing people disappeared from here, didn't they?"

"Alastair Chelon disappeared from Black Hole Lake on August seventeenth," Lucy recited, "sometime between six and nine p.m. He worked at the factory, you know. I bet that's how he got exposed to the Nucralose so early."

They hurried along the water's edge, over a rocky outcropping and into a thicket.

"I still say going to the factory is a bad idea." Milo grunted as he hopped over a rotting log.

"Think of it as an adventure," said Lucy. "Like going to the moon. Was going to the moon a bad idea?"

"Maybe." Milo slapped a bug on his neck. "People don't seem to go there any more."

Lucy frowned. "Well, they should."

"Factories are unsafe," said Milo. "Something could fall and smash your face in. Or you could trip into a big vat and melt your face off."

"You seem really concerned about my face," said Lucy. FONCH. She looked down to find a large Nu Co. cup stuck to her foot. A crumpled Nurro Churro wrapper lay next to it. "Carnival trash."

Milo looked around. "So somebody *is* out here."

"At least it's not a bear."

Milo gulped.

The sun disappeared behind a roil of Pacific Northwestern grey as they ducked under the twisted roots of a fallen cedar.

Up ahead, dangling from a mossy branch, was another bird feeder. Perched on the contraption, its magnificent striped wings extended for balance, was an owl. *Déjà vu.* It swivelled its head around backwards to look at Milo and Lucy.

"That's the same bird we saw before," said Milo. "I'm sure of it."

The owl shook its feathers, then leapt from its perch and dived at the children. They squealed and ducked, their hands covering their heads. Swooping up at the last second, the bird screeched mockingly and disappeared into the treetops.

"This is starting to feel personal," Lucy groused.

"The freaky magpie's over there," Milo pointed.

The black and white bird sat in a squat tree, hopping impatiently. It squawked, flew up to a higher branch and squawked again.

Lucy ran at it to scare it off, but she slipped in a puddle of something slick and landed painfully on her tailbone with a SQUISH. "Ow!" she yowled.

She clambered to her feet. "Ugh." The back of her jeans was covered in clear, snot-like sludge.

Milo inspected the puddle. "This is like the slime we saw at the medical tent."

Lucy's chest felt tight. "Whoever's out here, they're in trouble."

The magpie cackled and took off deeper into the woods, skimming the tops of the ferns.

Lucy noticed a glistening trail under the bird's flight path. "It's leading that way."

They followed the slime through a gooseberry bush and into a darkened copse. Milo raised a shaky finger towards a wooden hut up ahead, camouflaged by perennials. Along its outer wall were darkened slits for birdwatchers to look through, undetected by wildlife.

"Bird blind," Lucy whispered.

A soft whimpering sound was coming from the

shack. Gingerly, Lucy bent down and grabbed an arm-sized stick from the forest floor. Milo did the same.

At her signal, they tiptoed along the soft ground towards the hut, the mournful sound growing louder. Outside the open doorway, a pair of worn and muddy boots lay askew on the forest floor. The shoes were overflowing with transparent slime.

Just visible inside the shadowy structure were two large, nearly human-looking feet, toes pointing skyward. The feet had an oozy sheen, and their overlong yellow toenails were growing longer by the second. Suddenly, the feet thrashed violently and their owner let out a pitiful moan. A moment later they were still again, the ball of each foot darker, the arch wider, the toes longer.

Cripe sandwiches.

Lucy gripped her improvised weapon and signalled for Milo to wait where he stood. He nodded curtly and raised his stick behind him like a golf club.

Lucy crept through the doorway and squinted through her dirty glasses, her vision slowly adjusting to the blind's dim interior. The dusty air smelled piney and vaguely sweet.

Lying across the cramped cabin floor was a large, hairy being. It lay on its back, distorted palms pressed into its eyes, its mouth drawn in an anguished grimace that revealed crooked lower fangs. A patchy grey beard was lost in the thick wiry fur creeping down its neck, shoulders, chest and legs. The remnants of denim and flannel clothing hung off its pot-bellied body. An empty cup of Nu Co. Cola lay at its side, along with a pair of broken drumsticks.

Lucy gasped. The rapidly deforming beast was none other than Steve Kozlowski, the drummer of The Sticky Six. Or, at least, it used to be.

Lucy gaped at the poor, tormented creature, her knees shaking with adrenalin. With a judder, Steve's face contorted until it was completely unrecognisable. His brow broadened and his bottom teeth jutted out towards his cheekbones. Lucy's stick slipped out of her hand and clattered on the wooden floor.

"S-S-S-Steve?" she stuttered.

The monster groaned like a sea lion, its eyes rolling back in his head. *I don't think Steve knows who I am right now...*

The creature tried to sit up, its face shifting hideously between human and beast. It faltered and fell back to the wooden floor. Grunting and snorting like an injured wildebeest, it rolled on to its back.

"Lucy?" Milo whispered from behind the outer wall. "What's going on in there?"

"I have to help him," she murmured. She reached into her slimy pocket and pulled out the packet of sweets.

"What are you doing?" Milo hissed.

She took out a flattened piece of chocolate, took a deep breath and tossed it at the creature's mouth.

The candy bounced off its blunt snout.

The monstrous figure contracted to the foetal position and howled.

Startled, Milo leapt into the tent, his eyes shut tight, screaming and swinging his stick in the air. "AAAAAAHHHHHHH!" Hitting nothing, he opened his eyes. His jaw dropped. "Bigwoof?"

Lucy nodded. "BIGWOOF."

The creature tried to rise again but stumbled.

Frantically, Lucy tossed another wad of chocolate, this time directly into the beast's open mouth.

The creature choked and clawed at its mighty throat.

"KKKRRRAAAAAOOOOOAAAAAAA-AHHH!" Its jaw unhinged, foamy spittle hitting Lucy and Milo's shins.

Holy hellhounds.

Milo dropped his stick, grabbed his awe-struck friend by the back of the shirt and yanked her out of the blind.

The monster tore after them, breaking through

the flimsy shack, sending splinters flying.

"GAAAH!" The kids raced back along the glistening path, through the sticky grove, slipping on puddles of slime, back towards Black Hole Lake.

"RRRRNNNNNGGGXXXX...WWHHH-RRRRGGG." Bigwoof whiffled after them, crashing and gnashing through the trees.

Lucy and Milo burst on to the lakeshore. The wind gathered and churned, steam rising and falling from the murky waters.

The towering beast stood at the treeline, fists clenched at its sides, its broad chest heaving in the swirling mist. It gazed upon the cowering companions like a grisly god and bellowed a formless haunting cry.

"KKKHHOOOOGGGGWWWWWAAA-WRRRRRRXXX!"

A loud CRACK sounded in the distance and the monster whipped around.

"Gunshot," said Lucy. "Fish, that was a gunshot!"

The monster growled and took off in the direction of the noise.

"Bigwoof, wait!" Lucy shouted. She took off after it without a second thought.

Milo slapped himself on the cheeks. "Of course her stupid monster is real." He swallowed his dismay and chased after her at top speed.

Lucy locked on to the abominable creature as it loped through the trees, over a hill and down towards a winding forest road. One thing was certain, this time she wasn't alone. Milo had seen everything too. Her heart soared. *No one will ever call me crazy again.*

Bigwoof snuffled viciously at the edge of an embankment. Lucy scrambled up the incline and hid behind a bush a few metres away. Milo slid into the foliage beside her.

A white van, similar to the one that had transported Carlos from the fair, raced down the road below the creature. Lucy and Milo dropped to the ground as Bigwoof beat its chest and screamed like a drowning pack of wolves.

The large vehicle skidded to a stop. The van door opened and Mr Dum and Mr Dummer stepped out on to the roadway. Each of them carried a large gun.

What are they— No!

BANG! Dummer fired and the mighty beast faltered, an orange tranquilliser dart sticking out of its chest. Another BANG, this time from Dum, and a pink dart punctured Bigwoof's thigh.

The beast wobbled, its vision going in and out of focus. Lucy watched in horror as it careened over the embankment's edge, sprawling out on the road below.

Milo held Lucy back from rushing over to help the creature. "Stay down," he insisted. "The clowns will see you. Let them deal with the monster."

"That's a person down there," she spat. "Not a monster."

Three more clowns jumped out of the van and surrounded the helpless hairy being. A drizzle of rain coated its coarse fur in droplets of crystal.

"Strap it in with the other one," ordered Dummer. He ripped off his wig and threw it on the ground, running a hand through his thinning hair. "You heard me," he barked. "Move!"

Mr Dum opened the back of the van and the other clowns hefted the creature inside. All the men piled into the vehicle and slammed the doors behind them. The engine started up.

"They're taking it to Nu Co." Lucy raced out from behind the bush and slid down the embankment.

"Wait!" Milo cried. He tumbled after her.

Lucy leapt on to the windowless rear of the vehicle and grasped the locked handle with both hands.

The van backed towards Milo, who hopped on, holding on to Lucy for dear life. No one got out of the vehicle to retrieve them. With all the commotion, Milo and Lucy hadn't been noticed.

The driver shifted into gear and drove off towards the factory.

"Here we go," Milo gulped, his eyes shut tightly.

"Here we go," said Lucy, her eyes open wide.

CHAPTER 14

Out of the Woods
and into the...

Lucy's teeth buzzed with the vibration of the van's motor. She strained to hold on to the door with every muscle in her body as Milo tightened his grip around her waist.

"That thing can't possibly be Steve," Milo whispered. "How is that possible?

"I told you," said Lucy. "It's the FOOD."

"There's no way..." Milo began. "I mean, how could... Maybe it ATE Steve?"

"Believe what you want," Lucy sighed.

The vehicle drove steadily, as though the driver was in no rush, as though there wasn't an inexplicable cryptocreature writhing inside, concealed from the rest of the normal, rational world by nothing but a pair of metal doors.

"Still think Bigwoof's a grolar bear?" Lucy muttered.

"Is now really the time for your inevitable 'I told you so'?" Milo grunted.

Lucy pressed her ear to the door to listen for the beast, but all she could hear was the incessant crunch of the dirt road beneath the tyres. She wondered if the Bigwoof had woken up yet, and worried that it may never wake again after all the tranquilliser darts the clowns had shot into it. Would it ever turn back into the man who played drums in her father's band? Or would it stay a monster forever?

Nu Co.'s private driveway cut through a vast blue orchard of sticky pines. At the end of the road lay the factory, a large brick building with a pyramidal smoke stack spewing puffs of brown smoke.

"We need to get off this thing soon," Lucy warned.

"If we jump, we'll end up splattered across the road," said Milo.

THOMP THOGGIDY.

Lucy heard a muffled sound inside the van. She leaned in and listened. "I think I hear it moving around in there," she said. After a moment of silence she leaned away. "Never mind. I guess it was nothing."

With a CRUNCH, the door bulged out as if struck by a cannon, right where Lucy's head had been, the white paint cracking open like the veins of an eyeball. Something had hit the door, hard, from the inside.

"Whoa!" The metal distended again and struck Milo's shoulder, nearly knocking them both off the vehicle.

Lucy and Milo heard the muffled sounds of shouting men as they picked up speed.

"We have to jump," Lucy urged.

Milo shook his head, arching his body away from a blow at his back. "We're going too fast."

"We don't have a choice." Lucy leaned out

and peered at the road ahead. "There's a big turn coming up. They'll have to slow down. We can do it then."

Milo glanced at the gravel racing below them. "Are you crazy? I mean, I know you're crazy, but are you nuts?"

"We've come too far to get caught now." She shifted her weight and made room for Milo to grab on to the handle. "Get ready."

As Lucy predicted, the van slowed as it rounded the corner, the beastly commotion within growing louder. Pushing her fear aside, she leapt from the vehicle to the orchard. She landed on her side and skidded into the trees, her fall cushioned by a mixed blessing of mud and pine needles.

Milo dived after her and rolled through the dirt as the van fishtailed around the bend.

He flopped down next to Lucy, sore and out of breath. "You're bleeding," he panted, looking at her elbows.

"So are you," Lucy grimaced. She gently

removed the pine needles sticking out of his roughed-up knees, then did the same to her arms.

"It's a wonder I have any skin left after today." Milo shook the gravel out of his loafers, which were scuffed beyond recognition.

They mucked their way through the soggy orchard. Each tree was covered in V-shaped gashes exposing blood-red wood beneath the pale, flaky bark. Black sap drained from the base of each V, seeping into buckets that had been nailed low to collect the sweet substance.

They reached the edge of the parking lot outside the grimy building where their fathers spent their working days. The words "Nu Co." had been painted above the front door in towering white letters. A shallow cement staircase led to a pair of double doors, beige like the ones at school. Lucy wondered how many times her father had crossed this bland threshold.

The van was parked haphazardly at the back of the building. Tyre marks on the cement suggested it had skidded to an abrupt stop. The rear doors had been ripped open by some furious force of nature. *Or supernature.*

There were no creatures, clowns or corporate officers in the vicinity.

"Where is everybody?" asked Milo.

"Inside, I guess." Lucy's brow furrowed. "How do we break in?"

"Why don't we try the front door?"

"The front door?" She laughed. "Now who's the crazy one?"

"You have a better idea?"

"Yeah." Lucy pushed her glasses up her nose. "Like, any idea."

"You underestimate the direct approach," said Milo. "All the workers like your dad are at the fair. The clowns are in the back with Bigwoof. I'll bet you ten thousand bucks nobody is watching the front door."

Lucy scanned the darkened windows. If anyone was in there, she could see no sign. But that didn't mean nobody was. She scratched her chin. "I guess it's worth a try."

They jogged up the steps, pausing at the top to steel their nerves. Milo grabbed the handle and pulled. It was unlocked.

"After you." He gestured for her to enter.

Lucy exhaled nervously and stepped inside.

The heavy door slammed behind them with a resonant CLANG.

They were on a grated platform overlooking the factory floor. The hum of electricity reverberated around them, the air thick with the saccharine scent of Nucralose.

The facility was big enough to house a jumbo jet, its high ceiling strewn with spinning industrial fans and translucent yellow skylights. A set of shiny metal tubes and pipes ran along the floor towards the centre of the room, neatly snaking around cauldrons, machines and conveyor belts, all leading to a massive copper vat as big as the above-ground swimming pool in Tex's backyard.

Lucy listened for voices, but heard nothing. It

seemed they were alone.

She and Milo descended the stairs towards a row of wide cylindrical vats with ladders running up each side. They looked shiny and new, as did much of the equipment they could see.

Lucy knocked on one of the vessels and heard a dull CLONG. She hopped on to the ladder.

"What are you doing?" asked Milo.

"I wanna see what this stuff looks like."

"Hurry up then. And don't fall in."

Inside the open cylinder, freshly harvested sap simmered in an early step along the surely fascinating journey to becoming an alternative pine sweetener. A large bubble forced its way to the surface, spritzing Lucy's cheeks with black goop.

"See anything interesting?" asked Milo.

"Nothing unexpected." She wiped her face with her sleeve and craned her neck to get a better sense of the massive space. At the far end of the room was a doorway labelled "SUBTERRANEAN STORAGE".

The basement. That looks promising. She slid down the ladder to the concrete floor.

"I know where to go," said Lucy.

Milo was staring uneasily at the ceiling.

"What's wrong?" said Lucy.

"I thought I saw a shadow on the skylight."

Lucy looked up, trying to spot whatever ill fortune would befall them next. She saw nothing. "Maybe it was that freaky owl again?"

"Maybe," said Milo. "There are cameras up there, by the way." He pointed to each of the high corners of the building.

"I wonder if some clown creep is watching us."

"I guess we'll find out."

They crept down aisle after aisle of giant silver equipment. Some gurgled while others buzzed with unseen purpose. At the centre of it all was the enormous copper vat, brewing beneath a large fan that swept up its rising steam in a ghostly vortex.

This is it. Lucy felt a shiver run down her spine.

The stuff that turns people into monsters. Before Milo could object, she scurried up the ladder on the side of the vat.

The contents of this vessel looked quite different from the dark, sappy substance from which it had been transformed. Stirred from below by some unseen force, it rippled like liquid gold. The eye-watering scent of pine was now masked by a buttery odour, like the popcorn they sold at the cineplex.

"This stuff is crazy," she said to Milo. "You've gotta see it."

"Get down from there before somebody spots us," he urged, nearly tripping over a steel-covered cable.

"Somebody already has," said a terse adult voice.

The kids turned in alarm as an undulating shadow emerged from behind a humming cylinder. A small woman appeared, dark hair pinned neatly atop her head, her long white lab coat billowing behind her in the industrial-fan-conjured breeze.

It was the doctor from the medical tent. "Step away from the product," she ordered.

The biggest clown they had seen yet marched out from behind a bottling station and headed towards Milo, who didn't seem to know which way to run.

Lucy gritted her teeth and jumped down with a THUD.

"I don't know how you podunks usually operate," said the fuchsia-haired henchman, in a voice that was higher than Lucy had expected, "but we don't appreciate intruders at this facility." A set of ridiculous green freckles adorned his rosy cheeks.

"Especially thieves," barked the tiny doctor.

"We're not thieves," said Milo.

"What the crud's a podunk?" asked Lucy.

The clown appeared to be confused by the question.

"What are you doing in here?" asked the doctor.

"Playing sardines," said Lucy.

"Lucy…" Milo whispered. His eyes were locked on the ceiling.

What is he staring at?

"I'll take these rugrats to the back office, Doctor Quittan." The clown grabbed Milo roughly by the collar.

"Fish!" said Lucy, reaching for him.

"Duck!" Milo squealed, covering his head with his hands.

"Why are they saying animals?" demanded Doctor Quittan.

With a loud crash, something big and yellow fell through the skylight, sending shards of metal and plastic into the vat of golden goo. A plume of steam rose from the cauldron and spiralled towards the ceiling, thick, and dark, and fast.

CHAPTER 15

Cauldron of Doom

A person-sized something had fallen through the skylight, but it hadn't fallen far – it was caught on a twisted windowpane, agitating the clouds of steam that concealed it from view.

"This is unacceptable!" seethed Doctor Quittan. "The product must not be contaminated." She stormed over to a panel near the cauldron and pressed a big green button.

There was a hiss and a whir as the ceiling fan kicked into high gear. The steam dispersed, revealing a very large banana dangling from the mangled skylight like a cocoon, legs flailing in mid-air.

Millepoids! Lucy gaped at the candy man in awe. *How the plop did he get up there?*

"Forget the children," Doctor Quittan barked at the clown. "The substance must be protected at all costs."

"Yes, Doctor!" The clown saluted. He released Milo and turned his focus to the pendulous banana and the bubbling vat directly below. "We've got a situation on the main floor involving the rogue agent," he spoke into his flower. "We need backup. Repeat, we need backup."

Liberated from the flustered clown, Milo yanked Lucy down an aisle of open containers outfitted with blinking dials and measures. He knocked on each one as they passed, trying to find one that rang hollow.

"In here," he said. He hopped over the side of a squat tank and ducked inside with a tinny BONG.

Lucy followed, and they stood on tiptoe to peek over the rim.

Above the vat of Nucralose, Millepoids kicked

his feet, twisting and turning in his loosening costume.

"Code red," the clown shouted into the flower on his chest. "I repeat, code red at beta location."

"What is Millepoids doing?" Milo whispered. "Does he *want* to fall in?"

"He can't possibly," said Lucy. "He knows what that stuff does." *If eating and drinking Nucralose turned Steve and Carlos into Bigwoofs, what would a whole vat of it do to Millepoids?*

The dangling candyman swung his legs high and then kicked low, squirming until his slender body, clad in black spandex, slid out of the bottom of the peel. He caught the banana suit with both hands and hung for just a moment, looked down at the simmering soup, and let go.

"No!" cried Lucy and Doctor Quittan, simultaneously but for different reasons.

"CODE RED!" barked the clown.

Millepoids landed in the cauldron with a sickening SPLOOSH. His yellow costume, freed by the sudden loss of weight, split and fluttered like a Jurassic butterfly to the factory floor.

"Why? Lucy choked. "Why did he do it?" She felt like she was going to be sick.

The sinister sweetener bubbled madly, pearls of syrup cascading on to the floor.

"Backup," the clown squeaked into his flower as he jumped aside to avoid the golden goop.

"Why aren't they going in after him?" Milo asked anxiously.

The doctor stared at the vat as if transfixed, her face frozen in awed anticipation. She, too, kept a cautious distance from the spilled substance.

"He's alive," Lucy gulped. "Listen."

A banging sound emanated from the giant cauldron, soft and sporadic. Millepoids was swimming around inside, though he hadn't surfaced.

"It's not possible…" said Milo.

The banging grew louder. Lucy had a feeling that something very bad was about to happen.

For the first time in her life, she hoped she was wrong.

With a resounding CLANG, a dripping, distorted hand gripped the copper rim. It was soon joined by another. Then another. And another.

Holy cripes.

And another.

"Unbelievable," Milo murmured.

All at once, an impossibly enormous beast rose from the shimmering stew and revealed itself, pulling itself up by eight long, spidery limbs. At last, it perched like a grim gargoyle at the edge of the cauldron. Six black eyes clustered on its brow above a snarling, wolfish snout. A coat of golden goo trickled down its hairy, bulbous body.

The blood drained from Lucy's face. *Spiderwoof.* The hideous thing that once was Mandy Millepoids, beloved Sticky Pines candyman, balanced on the balls of its freakish feet, raised its misshapen head and howled – an enraged cry that reverberated across every surface on the factory floor.

Lucy and Milo crouched and covered their anguished ears until the walls of their hiding place ceased vibrating.

Catching her breath, Lucy peeked back over the edge of the tank. *What have these quackheads done?*

Steely-eyed, Doctor Quittan approached the creature. "Mr Millepoids," she said with a confident smile. "I assure you, we mean you and your friends no harm. Come, let us discuss this situation like civilised people."

The monster snorted in her general direction and surveyed the factory floor with its many glistening eyes.

"We-we are quite close to getting to the bottom of this little mishap," the doctor stammered. "The others will be released as soon as we have all the information we need, I assure you."

The corners of the beast's mouth stretched into a terrible grimace as it made an unearthly guttural sound.

Lucy realised with a chill that it was laughing.

The many-limbed creature leapt high into the air and landed with a THUD on a wide rectangular machine with black tubes sticking out the back. With a vicious kick, it sent a panel flying, exposing a series of wires and blinking lights. Lucy forgot to breathe as the monster tore into the machine's innards, scraps flying everywhere.

"Stop this tantrum at once," commanded the doctor. "We can help you. All of you. Let's work together to—"

Quittan shrieked as the ghastly being parkoured off the foamy cauldron and landed on a crouch on the floor before her, its front legs poised above its head like a black widow about to strike. Its beastly face oozed with anger, a low growl emanating from a throat large enough to swallow the doctor whole.

"Back off!" Quittan's high-pitched henchman charged at the creature. The clown immediately slipped on the banana peel costume and skidded head-first into the side of the vat. BOMPHSQUEEEEEE. He slumped uselessly to the floor, leaving a streak of white face paint along the shiny copper.

The Millepoids monster chuckled and leapt on to a tall vessel across the aisle from a terrified Lucy. It seemed to wink at her with three of its eyes as it thrust its talons into the cold steel, penetrating the container as though it were made of paper. Brown liquid squirted out of each hole, splattering the machinery around it.

Satisfied, the monster bounded off to attack a series of blue tubes depositing something into a trough. With one swipe, the tubes were ripped in half, spewing a fizzy substance that smelled like rancid lemons.

Lucy sank into the tank and huddled next to Milo, who was cradling his filthy face between his knees.

Outside their hiding place they heard the sound of shattering glass followed by a grotesque cackle.

Lucy patted Milo's head. "It'll be OK," she said, not at all sure that it would, for any of them, ever again.

Milo rocked back and forth. "My dad wouldn't let any of this happen on purpose, I know he wouldn't."

"Whatever he did or didn't do," said Lucy, "we have to find the others. The people they've been holding here. We've gotta help them."

A fire alarm rang out and shouting voices filled the room.

"That'll be the backup," muttered Lucy.

The vibrations of many pounding feet echoed around the factory floor. There was a TWHACK and a yelp as a human body hit a nearby vessel.

"Time to go." Lucy helped Milo to his feet.

The factory was in chaos. Ten clowns in smeared make-up and combat boots charged at the creature, their tranquilliser guns raised.

The steam from the vat was now joined by the smoke of several electrical fires. The sprinkler system activated and water rained down from the ceiling, slickening the floor and causing the clowns to slide about pathetically.

The Spiderwoof was seated at the edge of the copper vat. It trailed a claw languidly inside, stirring the hazardous goop.

"You're surrounded," said an amplified voice. It was Mr Fisher, speaking into a loudspeaker several yards away from the central cauldron. He signalled for the clowns to keep their distance from the beast. "End this now," Fisher continued. "You're only putting yourself and the others in jeopardy."

Millepoids sank his talons into the edge of the copper container, scrunching the metal like cardboard. A trickle of glistening syrup ran down the side and on to the floor.

"Get back," Fisher barked at the clowns. "Everyone, get back!"

The goons started to back away. Then a shot rang out – one of the trigger-happy clowns had fired without warning. A split second later a barrage of shots sounded, one after another,

POP POP POP!

Millepoids bellowed as he was bombarded with colourful darts. He tried to shake them off but was immediately hit by two more. He teetered on the edge of the cauldron, clutching it to keep himself upright.

"We need to go now!" Lucy hoisted herself out of the tank.

Milo clambered after her and they made a beeline for the back of the factory, ducking behind tables and bottling machines to keep out of sight. They crouched behind a conveyor belt, not far from the basement door. Two clowns, one with green hair and one with yellow, stood at either side of the doorway, tranquilliser guns in hand.

"There's no way past them," said Lucy.

Milo stiffened. "I can think of one way," he said. He squeezed Lucy's shoulder. "Go find the others. Don't waste this chance."

Before she could ask him what on the round blue Earth he was planning to do, Milo darted into the middle of the aisle.

"Hey, bozos," he shouted, waving his hands in the air.

"Is that a kid?" yelped the clown with the haystack hair.

"Where did he come from?" shouted the green one.

Milo turned on his heel and ran towards the pandemonium at the centre of the floor.

"Get back here!" shouted the haystack clown.

They took off after him, racing past Lucy, who marvelled in dismay at her friend's sacrifice. Milo dodged the buffoons, skidding across the slippery floor and out of sight.

Fish, what have you done?

"That's my son!" cried Mr Fisher into the megaphone. "Get him out of here!"

More shots rang out and Lucy heard the Millepoids monster wail pitifully. Then came the slow, creaking sound of buckling metal.

"He's tearing it open," shouted a voice.

"Run," shouted another.

"Milo!" shouted Lucy.

But it was too late. Millepoids fell, taking the wall of the copper vat with him. With a horrendous RIIIIIIIIIIIP, a cascade of pure Nucralose surged from the container, engulfing the stampeding clowns in a swell of syrup.

The noxious wave gurgled towards Lucy. "Milo," she cried again, but couldn't find him in the crowd.

Did he get away?

She had no choice but to run.

With no plans of slowing down, she slammed her body into the crash bar on the basement door, thrusting herself into darkness.

CHAPTER 16

Fuzzy Findings

Lucy slammed the door and held it shut. A trickle of golden goo seeped through the gap at the bottom. She spread her legs wide to avoid it, one foot wedged into the corner of the windowless cement hallway in which she now stood. She was safe, for now.

The same could not be said for everyone on the factory floor. There were a dozen people out there exposed to pure Nucralose, Milo among them.

Is he a Bigwoof? A Spiderwoof? Will he even know who I am any more?

Carefully, Lucy side-stepped the goo. She

pulled out the battered packet of chocolates Millepoids had given her and peeked inside. Amid the chaos, the candies had been smooshed into a single dense mound. It did not look appetising. *But maybe it can help the others.* She wasn't sure that all the candy in the world could cure Millepoids.

Shaking her nerves out through her fingers, she ventured down the hall to a staircase that descended into bright white light.

Quiet as an owl in flight, she crept down into a high-ceilinged warehouse, empty of clowns, doctors or other members of the Nu Co. cryptocorporate machinery. Rows of fluorescent strip lights flickered and hummed overhead. The room was filled with rows of plastic-wrapped cardboard boxes stacked several metres high. Each was enthusiastically labelled: "NuCotton Candy!", "Nu Co. Cola!", "Now With All-new Nucralose!" The eerie clown mascot mocked Lucy over and over from every side.

On the other end of the warehouse was a

wooden door with the word "PRIVATE" stencilled over it in ominous red letters.

I'll bet that's where they are.

Lucy tiptoed to the nearest row of packaged products. There was just enough space between the boxes and the wall for a smallish person to uncomfortably squeeze into, which she was, so she did. She shimmied through the cramped space until she reached a central aisle. Now it was a matter of crossing to the other side of the room unseen.

As soon as Lucy stepped into the aisle, the PRIVATE door swung open. Two men, a stranger in a lab coat and a very shabby-looking clown, entered the warehouse, deep in conversation. Lucy dropped to the floor and slid under a pile of wood pallets. She spat out a dust bunny and peered between the slats.

"Thank you for your assistance." The older man in the white coat spoke softly, assuredly. His hair was close-cropped and uniformly white, his skin a deep, unnatural tan, speckled with age.

"That weatherman is more feisty than he looks," said the clown. Lucy recognised the Captain's voice at once. His red nose was gone, as was his orange wig. Remnants of his blue-painted smile were still visible on his sweaty cheeks. "Tell me, Doctor Vink," he sniffed, "how much longer are we going to be stuck in this backwoods town?"

"As long as it takes," replied the doctor.

"Hmph," grunted the Captain. "I'm starting to feel like an overgrown babysitter, and I don't like it."

"Perhaps you should speak with Mr Fisher."

"Maybe I will. I've had enough of this hillbilly enterprise. I say dissect them all, strip the land and be done with it."

Lucy flushed with anger. *So they really are planning on dissecting people.*

"You have a problem with the fresh air, Mr Murl?" asked Doctor Vink.

"The air, the ugly trees, the creepy locals," the

clown responded. "It's the whole town. Nothing but freaks."

Doctor Vink looked bemused. "A wise man once said, there is a great deal to be gained in uncommon places where no one is watching."

"As long as I get what's mine," Murl chortled. "And that's all of it."

Lucy gritted her teeth. *These guys might be the biggest clods I've encountered today. And that's saying something.*

The men ascended the staircase, their laughter fading as they disappeared into the hall. Lucy seized her chance and sprinted over to the PRIVATE door, shutting it gently behind her.

Whoa. What is this place? She was in a long underground tunnel made of stone. The cool air smelled faintly of eggs.

The arched ceiling was a mosaic of glittery stones in shades of grey, green, yellow and pink, arranged in swirling geometric patterns. A row of antique light bulbs dangled from fraying cloth cords, giving off a warm glow. The light faded into darkness before Lucy could make out the tunnel's end. Large wooden panels on tarnished sliding tracks were set along the walls. *Is this some kind of dungeon?*

Gingerly, she descended a shallow stone staircase, each step bowed at the centre as if worn by centuries of footsteps. The bottom step was inlaid with a set of glyphs, spelling out something in a strange language Lucy had never seen before.

She pulled the iron loop handle of the nearest door. It slid open with a creak, triggering a set of fluorescent lights to seize fitfully into illumination.

Fisher's people had restyled the ancient room as some sort of office. There was a long desk along the wall, atop which sat two computers and a CCTV monitor. A pair of swivel chairs sat askew, as if they had been quickly vacated. On the other side of the room was a freestanding whiteboard covered in chemical equations, DNA sequences and question marks. At the top, somebody had translated the glyphs Lucy had seen on the stairs: "Beware the Pretenders".

Curiouser and curiouser.

There was motion on the monitor. Lucy leaned on the desk to examine it, accidentally knocking over an empty can of original-formula Sticky Sweet Soda with her elbow. It hit the floor with a BANG and rolled clatterously over the cobblestones.

She snapped around to check the open doorway. Had anyone heard? She held her breath for several seconds. Nobody came.

They're still busy with Millepoids. But for how long?

The CCTV displayed footage of a big white-walled room outfitted with IV stands and other medical equipment. Large, sturdy metal beds lined the walls, all bolted to the stone floor. Six of the beds were occupied. Sitting on a bed closest to the window, a woman in a mint-green hospital gown stared into the camera, looking quite cross.

Mrs Stricks!

Lucy raced into the hallway, her footsteps echoing in the stale air. *Where is she?* She slid open the next door and found a small, darkened chamber. It contained nothing but a couple of folding chairs and a video camera on a tripod. The camera faced a large rectangular window set into the wall.

On the other side of the big window, Mrs Stricks gazed sadly in Lucy's direction. Her short hair was mussed and unwashed, her gaunt face covered in a sparse layer of wiry Bigwoof hair, her eyes droopy with fatigue. Electrodes stuck out of her chest and head, connected to a blinking machine at her side.

Lucy jumped up and down to get her teacher's attention. Mrs Stricks scratched her nose obliviously. *She can only see herself*, Lucy realised. *This isn't a window, it's a two-way mirror.*

Tex's dad, Serge, knew about all kinds of spy stuff (though he insisted he wasn't one).

Serge had once explained to Lucy how two-way mirrors worked. The trick was that one side of the glass needed to be dark and one side needed to be light. If a person looked at the glass from the light side, they would see their own reflection, like a mirror. If a person looked at the glass from a dark room, they could see through it like a window, while remaining hidden from the person on the other side. If both rooms were light, however, both sides of the two-way glass would be transparent, like a regular window.

Lucy found the light switch by the door and flicked it on.

Mrs Stricks stood up, a shocked expression on her furry face. She squinted. "Lucy?" she seemed to say.

"Mrs Stricks." Lucy waved her hands and mouthed her words deliberately. "I'm coming to get you!"

Mrs Stricks shook her head. "You have to get out of here. It's not safe."

But Lucy had already darted back into the

hallway, hauling boots to the next door.

She yanked on the handle but the panel wouldn't budge. The door had been latched with a heavy padlock.

Clamsauce. I need a key.

Racing back to the office, she searched the desk, sifting through neatly filed papers, calculators and boxes of granola bars. *Key, key, where's the flippin' key?*

She was on the brink of giving up when she picked up a small matchbox from the Banana Slug Saloon. Something metal rattled inside. *Aha!* She slid it open and dropped a silver key into her palm.

She careened back to the locked door. Hands shaking, she struggled to insert the key. At last, the padlock opened with a CLICK.

The massive panel opened and the sharp scent of antiseptic wafted into the tunnel, stinging Lucy's eyes.

"What are you doing here?" Mrs Stricks gasped. A thinning stripe of white hair ran from her anxious forehead to the tip of her nose, like a badger. She gaped at her student as if unsure she was real. Lucy noticed that Mrs Stricks's canine teeth looked longer than usual. "You have to get out of here," the teacher insisted. "It's not safe."

"I'm not going anywhere unless you go with me," said Lucy. She lurched forward and gave Mrs Stricks a big squeeze.

Mrs Stricks embraced Lucy, her arms shaking.

"Who's there?" croaked a voice from the far side of the room. An emaciated man sat up in his bed, his shoulders and neck covered in a mottled coat of brown and black. "No more tests, please. Not today."

"It's not the doctor, Alastair," said Mrs Stricks.

"Is it pizza?" he asked.

"It's never pizza," snapped Mrs Stricks. She daubed her forehead with the back of her hairy hand, her palm dark like a monkey's paw. "This is Lucy Sladan. Silas's daughter."

"The one who's into aliens?" He chuckled painfully. "It figures."

"You're Alastair Chelon, the factory worker," Lucy exclaimed. "People have been looking for you for weeks."

"It's nice to be noticed," Chelon smiled.

"You look an absolute mess," said Mrs Stricks. "What's happened to you?"

"What's happened to me?" said Lucy. "What's happened to *you*? Are you all right?"

"I've…" Mrs Stricks ran her tongue over her oversized teeth, "been better."

"You look better than you did yesterday," grunted Chelon. "When you almost bit my head off before they restrained you."

Lucy looked around the room and noted that all the steel beds had thick straps at each end, one for each arm and leg. *These aren't regular hospital beds, these beds were made for Bigwoofs. Fisher knew about this all along.*

"We need to get you out of here before Fisher comes back," said Lucy.

"We're not prisoners," said Mrs Stricks.

"You're not?" said Lucy, genuinely perplexed.

"But, this place…" She gestured to the hallway. "It's like a dungeon. The door was locked. Nobody knew where you were!"

"It's for our own safety," said Mrs Stricks, anxiously pulling at the hair on her chin, "and the safety of others. We … we keep turning into…" Her voice cracked, tears welling in her eyes.

"Bigwoofs," said Lucy.

"I was going to say 'monsters'," Mrs Stricks sniffed.

"It won't stop," sighed Chelon. "Every time they bring us back to normal, we change again. It could happen at any moment."

"How can eating Nucralose turn people into monsters?"asked Lucy.

"Fisher doesn't know." Chelon sat up delicately and draped his skinny legs over the side of the bed. "But he's trying to find out." His furry limbs were covered in bruises and welts. Dark circles shadowed his eyes. "Or, at least, he says he is," he added darkly.

"All we know is that the Nucralose sneaks up on you," said Mrs Stricks. "It builds up in your system over time. First you feel hot, then you start to tingle all over. Then – well." She waved a hand over her body.

"Hairy and scary, as it were," said Chelon.

"Mr Fisher has assured us he and his ... doctors," Mrs Stricks's nostrils flared angrily, "have been working on a cure. But they don't seem to be any closer to finding one."

"We're starting to think they're not really trying." Chelon leaned against the wall with a grunt.

Mrs Stricks grabbed Lucy by the shoulders. "Where's Esther? Does she know you're here?"

"The Other Mrs Stricks is safe," Lucy assured her. "Mr Millepoids found her before Fisher did. I haven't seen her since she saved me and Milo from being attacked by a bear."

"Excuse me?" said Mrs Stricks, aghast.

"She was a Bigwoof at the time," said Lucy.

"She was?" Mrs Stricks looked horrified. "In

public?" She sat and pressed her palms into her eyes and rocked back and forth. "No, no, no, this can't be happening."

Chelon stood, weakly. "Where is Mandy now?"

"Mr Millepoids is upstairs," Lucy spoke rapidly. "He fell into a vat of Nucralose and turned into a big ugly Spiderwoof."

"Bigwoof, Spiderwoof," Chelon chuckled. "I like this kid."

"We have to do something," Lucy urged. "Fisher threw a carnival today. They're feeding Nucralose to everyone. He's trying to turn the whole town into Bigwoofs."

Mrs Stricks stood, suddenly filled with teacherly authority. "He did WHAT?" she growled.

Lucy took a startled step backwards.

"That explains the new additions." Chelon eyed the four unconscious occupants strapped to the beds around them. They were all full-Bigwoofs. At least one of them was snoring.

He squinted at the nearest monster, which had eyelashes about a mile longer than any of the others. "Is that Carlos Felina, the weatherman?"

The beast's eyelashes fluttered as if in response.

"I thought I recognised that face," Chelon mused. "He looks better when he's clean-shaven."

Lucy gingerly approached the Carlos creature, a pink tongue lolling out the side of his toothy mouth. "Will he bite me?"

"Probably not," Chelon shrugged. "He's heavily drugged."

Lucy reached out and touched his face. Carlos's lip quivered in an involuntary snarl and her hand shot back.

In the next bed, a pot-bellied creature was snoring away. He was smaller than the others, almost human-sized. His blankets were covered in thick, wiry hair, which was shedding from his body in chunks, his ruddy flesh emerging beneath the fuzz.

"Steve Kozlowski," Lucy exclaimed. "We saw him running around as a Bigwoof in the woods."

"How many people saw him?" Mrs Stricks demanded.

"Just me and Milo," Lucy explained. "You know, Fisher's son. He's nice. Not like his dillweed dad. He's in trouble now too. Everyone upstairs got turned into Bigwoofs, or worse."

Mrs Stricks looked like she might have a heart attack.

Chelon shuffled over to Steve's bed. "Huh. Take a look at this, Twyla. The effect seems to be wearing off faster than normal." He exchanged a meaningful look with Mrs Stricks. "Much faster."

Mrs Stricks rushed over, yanking her IV stand along with her. "You're right," she said. "How is this possible?"

The chocolate. Lucy triumphantly held up the smashed paper packet. "Mr Millepoids gave me this. He said it's a cure." She pointed to the shedding creature. "I gave one to Steve.

I thought Millepoids might be nuts, but I think his chocolate might actually work." She handed the packet to Mrs Stricks.

"Oh sweet Susan." Mrs Stricks eagerly opened the package. "That man is a genius, I've always said it." She shoved a hunk of mushed candy in her mouth.

Chelon whistled. "Mandy, Mandy, so handy with candy."

"I'll bet Esther had a hand in this," said Mrs Stricks, still chewing. "She's quite good in the kitchen, you know."

Lucy glanced anxiously at the open door. "Everyone needs to eat, and fast. We have to escape before the clowns come back."

Mrs Stricks tossed the packet to Chelon, who caught it fumblingly with one hand.

"We have to tell the world about this," Lucy continued. "Carlos works for the news. He can put it on TV as soon as we get out of here."

"Oh, Lucy," said Mrs Stricks. "No. Absolutely not."

Shmuhuh? "Why the flip not? Everyone needs to know what happened here. It's like a messed-up miracle. Better than aliens, even!"

Alastair Chelon nearly choked on his hunk of sweet medicine.

"Lucy," said Mrs Stricks, her tone severe, "listen to me very carefully. You cannot tell anyone what you have seen. No one. Do you understand me?"

"No," said Lucy, "I don't."

"There are things about Sticky Pines that you don't understand," said Mrs Stricks, choosing her words carefully.

"You're saying too much," Chelon warned.

"What do you mean?" Lucy fumed. "Mr Fisher turned human beings into actual monsters with his crazy formula. He's a madman. He put the whole town in danger ON PURPOSE. Why would he do that? We have to stop him, and the only way to do that is to tell the truth."

Mrs Stricks shook her head. "Listen to me,

Lucy," she insisted. "Drawing attention to Sticky Pines will put us all at risk. You must trust me. I beg you. Nobody can find out what happened here."

"But ... why?" said Lucy.

"I am inclined to agree with the patient," said an elderly voice coming from the open doorway.

Everyone froze.

The venerable Doctor Vink strode coolly into the medical room, clipboard in hand. "Publicity, at this juncture, would be detrimental to our endeavours." Four clowns limped into the chamber behind him carrying the listless, exquisitely weird body of Mandy Millepoids.

The poor banana man was covered in tranquilliser darts. Though hairy and misshapen, he was much smaller than when Lucy had seen him last. They hoisted his gangly frame on to an empty bed, strapped his many arms and legs down and began hooking him up to a series of electrodes.

Mr Fisher entered behind them, his trousers

stained to the knee with syrup. He guided a sticky and dishevelled Milo into the room by the back of the neck.

"You're OK," said Lucy, melting with relief. "And you're not a Bigwoof. How—"

"There you are!" said Milo, too brightly. "I tell you," he said to his father, "she's got no sense of direction. It's a maze down here. No wonder she got 'lost'."

"Thank you, son," said Mr Fisher. "Next time, leave out the finger quotes. You can go now."

"But, Dad, I really think—"

"Go upstairs," his father demanded. He cleared his throat. "These gentlemen will see you there safely," he added more softly.

Fisher snapped his fingers and the dishevelled Dums stood at either side of the boy.

Milo gestured at Lucy. "What about her?"

"She will be with you shortly," said Mr Fisher. "But first, we need to have a little chat."

With that, the clowns escorted Milo out the door.

"Everything will be OK, I promise," Milo said over his shoulder as he disappeared into the tunnel.

He had been wrong about so many things up to this point. Lucy hoped this wasn't one of them.

"I will leave you to your patients, doctor," said Mr Fisher.

"Of course," nodded Doctor Vink. "Will you be needing any assistance with the girl?" He peered at Lucy in a way that made her skin prickle.

"That won't be necessary." Fisher placed a heavy hand on Lucy's shoulder. "Shall we?" It was not a question.

He gave Lucy a push towards the door. She stiffly complied, glancing back at Mrs Stricks.

The remaining clowns were busy strapping the twitching Millepoids to the bed.

Mrs Stricks frowned as she seemed to decide something. She yanked on one of the wires, disconnecting an electrode from her temple. Doctor Vink looked up from his clipboard as the machine at her side beeped in alarm.

What is she doing?

A clown rumbled the door panel shut in Lucy's face.

CHAPTER 17

Tunnel Vision

Mr Fisher escorted Lucy into the office at the head of the tunnel and shut the heavy door behind them. Lucy plopped down in a swivel chair in front of the equation-strewn whiteboard and kicked her feet while she considered her options. She had none.

Fisher sat opposite her with his back to the ransacked desk. The empty can Lucy had knocked to the floor lay at his feet. He picked it up, crushed it down to a fraction of its size and tossed it into a small wire bin.

"Are you pleased with what you've done to my factory?" he said.

"I want a lawyer." Lucy crossed her arms.

"You're not under arrest."

"Then can I go?"

"I'm not a policeman," he said. "I'm the owner of this facility and you're trespassing on my property."

Lucy bit her lip to stop herself from saying something she might regret. "I would like to speak to my parents, please."

"Again." He folded his hands in his lap. "I'm not a policeman."

Lucy's toes went cold.

"You know," he leaned forward, "it's unusual for Milo to take such a liking to new friends so quickly." He frowned. "It seems you've had quite an outsize influence on him. My son has never disobeyed me before today. When I saw him up there, looking like he'd been through a war, about to be attacked by that *thing*, I ... well, I've never been more frightened in my life."

Lucy fidgeted, glowering at the floor. She almost felt bad for Mr Fisher. *Almost*. She would have felt worse, if he wasn't the one responsible for all this craziness in the first place…

"We just wanted to know what you were hiding out here," she said. "We wanted to know the truth."

"You know," said Fisher, "you and I are much more alike than you realise."

"I doubt that. I'm not turning people into monsters."

"Is that what you think I'm doing?"

Ugh. What's the deal with this dingus? "I know what your Nucralose does to people. I've seen it with my own eyes."

"Pity you don't have a photograph to document what you saw."

Lucy had never before felt such a strong urge to punch someone in the face. *Filthy. Flippin'. Photoshopper.*

"Those people you've been keeping here," she said, "and sticking with needles and electrodes, *they* know what you did."

"And what are the chances, would you say,

that those … people," he emphasised the word, "will discuss this with anyone else?"

Lucy opened her mouth to speak, then closed it. Mrs Stricks had insisted that they couldn't tell anyone what had happened. *What was that about? Why is adult logic so infuriating?* Lucy was confused, one of her least favourite feelings.

Mr Fisher leaned forward. "How much do you think you know about your little town, Lucy?"

She scowled. "More than you do."

"Are you sure? I find it's possible to get a much clearer view of things from an outsider's perspective." He wandered over to the whiteboard, pondering the equations and glyphs scrawled upon it. "Fascinating, isn't it? How little we know about the world around us. About biology, chemistry, the universe itself."

"It's a real conundrum," mumbled Lucy.

"Milo has told me about your interest in the supernatural."

"Has he?" Lucy wondered how often Milo had spoken about her to his father.

"I admire your curiosity," Fisher continued. "And your tenacity. You never give up." He smiled tightly. "Whenever something strange happens, Lucy Sladan is there, causing trouble."

"The only trouble in Sticky Pines is you and your evil company."

"Despite what you may think, I had nothing but good intentions when I came out here. I'm a businessman, nothing more."

"Baloney."

"Nucralose," he rapped one of the chemical equations on the whiteboard with a knuckle, "was supposed to be the safest, most lucrative alternative sweetener on the market."

"Buh-loney."

"Instead, I found something much more intriguing." Mr Fisher crossed the room and perched on the edge of the desk. "Sticky Pines, it turns out, is just full of mysteries."

A burst of movement on the surveillance screen at his side showed some sort of struggle in the medical room. Lucy watched out of the corner of her eye, hoping Fisher wouldn't notice.

"The sap of the sticky pine tree is an extraordinary substance," he continued. "It could have so many applications, from nutrition to construction, to medicine, to warfare. If harnessed by someone with creativity and vision, it could advance the human species as we know it."

Lucy did not like the tone of his voice.

"Before we arrived," Fisher continued, "Sticky Pines was a tiny, forgotten corner of the world. Now it's been noticed. *You've* been noticed."

On the monitor, things were getting real in the medical room. Doctor Vink was lying on the floor, along with the clowns who had been assisting him. The previously unconscious beastly patients stumbled about groggily. Lucy clenched her fists. *Come on, guys, get out of there!*

"Something still puzzles me," said Mr Fisher. "You may have noticed that despite my exposure to Nucralose, I have not suffered any ill effects."

"That's not special," said Lucy. "Milo didn't either. Neither did most of the people at the fair."

"No one in my security team was affected either."

"Good for them." Lucy brushed a lock of sweaty hair away from her forehead. "Turning into a monster looks pretty gross."

"And hazardous to your health," said Fisher. "To survive such a transformation, a person would have to be *unnaturally* resilient to bodily harm."

Lucy's skin prickled with anger. "If it's so hazardous, why did you feed this crazy monster juice to the whole town?"

"Throwing the carnival was a risk I had to take in order to confirm my suspicions," he explained. "And because I have taken this risk," he took a step towards her, "I have uncovered an uncomfortable truth about Sticky Pines."

"What truth is that?" asked Lucy.

"There's something different about the people

who turned," said Fisher. "Something not right."

"Not right?"

"What if I told you," Fisher pointed over her head, "that the people in that room were monsters long before I came to town?"

"I ... huh?" *This guy is loony balloony.*

"My carnival flushed them out of hiding," Fisher continued, energised, "but I think there are more."

"More what?"

"More of *them*." He crouched down to her level, too close.

The room suddenly felt stuffy. Lucy pulled at the collar of her shirt.

"The teacher. The weatherman. The factory worker. The candyman. I don't know what they are," said Fisher, "but your friends in there are not human."

"Not human?" Lucy laughed, perplexed. "Then what are they?"

"That's a very good question. Oh, they look

like us, that's for sure, inside and out."

Lucy thought queasily of all the medical tests he must have performed on Mrs Stricks and Alastair Chelon.

"But they are *not us.*" A sneer crept on to Fisher's lip. "They're just pretending to be."

Lucy glanced up at the mysterious glyphs on the whiteboard: "Beware the Pretenders." Is this what those symbols meant? *But no, that's not possible...*

"Don't you see, Lucy?" Fisher continued, stepping ever nearer. "Everything you've seen today proves one thing: there's nothing wrong with my Nucralose, there's something wrong with Sticky Pines."

Lucy felt like her throat was being strangled from within.

"It's an incredible discovery, don't you think?" said Fisher.

She laughed nervously. "Snakes alive, dude, you're crazier than I am."

"How strange." Fisher cocked his head. "I

thought you of all people would be excited to learn about my theory."

"Those Bigwoof people are just people," said Lucy. "I've known them my whole life. They have neighbours and students and bosses and customers. They have friends." Then she remembered what Mrs Stricks had said: *"There are things about Sticky Pines that you don't understand." But no, she couldn't have meant...* "I mean, if they're not human, what are they?"

"That's what I plan to find out." Fisher placed his hand on the arm of her chair.

Lucy jumped up and backed against the knobbly stone wall.

Fisher moved to block the exit. "From everything I've witnessed, you, my dear, seem to be at the centre of this unfortunate hurricane. Whenever something strange happens, Lucy Sladan is there, getting in the way."

"I just wanted to learn the truth," she said hoarsely.

"I told you we were more alike than you

realised." Fisher's smile did not reassure her. "What I haven't been able to figure out," he kept pace with Lucy as she inched over to the desk, "is how you managed to resist the effects of Nucralose."

"I..." She swallowed. "I didn't eat any."

"Let's remedy that, shall we?" Fisher reached into the inside pocket of his black blazer and pulled out a vial filled with golden syrup.

Lucy felt ill.

"This version of Nucralose is brand new. It's still untested, but I think it should do the trick." He wiggled the flask of glittering goo. "Would you like to be the first to try it?"

Lucy clutched the desk, her arms behind her back. "I'm not hungry," she croaked.

Mr Fisher pulled the stopper out of the vial. "I'm afraid I must insist."

The sweet scent filled Lucy's nostrils, so strong she nearly gagged. She made a break for the door.

Mr Fisher caught her by the wrist.

"Hold still." He tilted the vial towards her lips.

Lucy screamed and twisted her arm until she broke his grip. Frantically, she scurried under the desk and huddled in the corner.

"What are you afraid of?" he asked, his voice growing louder. "Being exposed for what you really are?"

"I don't know what you're talking about," Lucy pleaded.

"I think you do." Fisher was too big to fit under the desk. He reached for her, but Lucy kicked his hands. He pulled the hem of Milo's baseball shirt so roughly she heard the fabric tear. At last, he yanked her out into the middle of the room. "What are they?" he demanded.

"Help!" Lucy yelled.

"What are *you*?" His grey hair was mussed, his cheeks flushed. "Let's find out." He shoved the glimmering substance towards Lucy's mouth. She turned her head and felt goo dripping down the side of her face.

She kicked Fisher in the shin as hard as she

could. He flinched and dropped the vial. It hit the stone floor and shattered, the sickly-sweet contents seeping into the dark spaces between the stones. He cursed and retrieved another one from his jacket.

Lucy tried to scramble away but Fisher grabbed her by the foot and dragged her. She clutched the leg of the desk, pulling it along with her and tipping the surveillance monitor on to the floor. The screen landed upside down and the image of the empty medical room flickered to darkness.

Fisher pinned Lucy to the hard, stony floor and tried to prise her mouth open. She bit his fingers as hard as she could.

"Aagh!" Fisher howled.

With a rumble, the heavy office door slid open.

CHAPTER 18

The Truth, or Something Like It

"Dad?" Milo was standing in the doorway, staring in shock at the pair grappling on the cold office floor.

"Milo!" Lucy cried, reaching for him.

"Dad, what are you doing?"

"Get out of here!" Mr Fisher took his hand off Lucy's face and waved his son away.

"Let her go." Milo ran into the room. "You're hurting her!"

Mr Fisher looked down at Lucy. Her face was red, tears streaming down her temples. He abruptly released her, then lumbered to his feet. He put the stopper in the vial and slipped it back into his pocket.

"You don't know what's at stake," he said to his son. "You have no idea what we're dealing with here."

Milo knelt by Lucy. "Are you OK?"

She nodded, her head throbbing.

Mr Fisher smoothed his hair and tightened his tie. "She's not what she seems," he explained. "She's dangerous."

"You're a liar." Lucy lunged towards Mr Fisher but Milo held her back by the arm. "You're the one who's dangerous."

The boy shook his head dazedly. "What's going on?"

"He tried to force-feed me Nucralose. He wanted to turn me into a monster." Lucy wiped the drying tears from her cheeks.

"I did no such thing," said Fisher.

His denial was spoken in a clear voice, his expression sincere enough that even Lucy was almost convinced. *Flip this fracking dillweed.*

"You didn't?" asked Milo. "You promise?"

"Of course," said Fisher. He opened his arms.

Milo took a step towards his father, but stopped when something crunched under his shoe. He examined the cobblestone floor, which glistened with experimental syrup and broken glass. "I don't believe you."

"Excuse me?" said Mr Fisher.

Lucy could feel his surprise and fury from across the room.

Milo's eyes were locked on the ground. "You knew what the Nucralose did from the beginning, didn't you?"

"This is all very complicated, son. We'll discuss it later. But first, get away from that girl. Now." Mr Fisher pointed to the floor beside him.

Milo glared at his father. "Do you expect me to follow orders without asking questions?"

"I expect you to do as you are told."

"I'm not one of your clowns." Milo's voice was shaky.

Mr Fisher's face reddened so much it was almost purple. "Do not take that tone with me."

"You can't control everything," said Milo. "You couldn't control it when Mom got sick, and you can't control everything now."

Mr Fisher looked as though he'd been punched in the gut.

"You've been lying to me from the moment we got here, haven't you?" said Milo. "What else have you lied about?"

"Someday," Fisher spoke softly, "you will understand. Everything I do, I do for you."

"Well, do me a favour and don't," Milo scoffed.

Fisher buttoned his suit jacket. "Let's deal with this at home." He reached for his son, but Milo pulled away.

Lucy watched them intently, wiping her raw nose with her sleeve. She had never seen Milo look so disgusted. She guessed the same was true for his father.

"Charming the youngsters the way you charmed the rest of us, eh, Fisher?" Mrs Stricks came into the room through the open door. Her face was now hair-free, her teeth once again back to their usual size. She scrutinised the tousled trio. "And I thought *I* looked like a dog's dinner. Everyone all right in here?"

"I think so." Lucy was suddenly hit by a wave of exhaustion. She caught a glimpse of the other recovering victims milling around in the tunnel. Miraculously, everyone appeared to be fully recovered. *I'll be slammed. What was in the chocolate?*

Mr Dum and Mr Dummer paced up and down the hall, yelling at one another in agitation.

Millepoids limped into the office, too tall for his hospital gown. His many limbs had been reduced back down to the usual four, but Lucy thought she spotted a few lumps beneath his flimsy attire. His bushy grey hair hung wetly around his shoulders.

Millepoids and Mrs Stricks looked and smelled like they needed a shower, but they appeared human.

Are they?

"Where is Doctor Vink?" Fisher demanded.

Mrs Stricks smiled sweetly. "He's taking a little nap." She cracked her knuckles. "And now, I believe it is time for us to go home."

"Not until we finalise the results of the study," said Fisher. "Everyone must return to the lab immediately."

Millepoids faced him squarely, nose to nose. "It's over, Fisher," he said. "You had your chance to fix this. We beat you to it. Your time is up."

"You've destroyed my entire facility." Fisher met his gaze with malice. "Nothing is over until I say it's over."

Millepoids bared his teeth, more grimace than grin. Lucy thought she heard a faint growl from deep within his throat.

"Why won't you let them leave?" asked Milo.

Mr Fisher didn't answer. He stood rigid, contemplating.

"Lucy!" Silas called to his daughter from the tunnel. "Get out of the way, my kid's in there," he yelled at Mr Dum.

The blue-haired buffoon hesitated but let him through. Silas burst into the office and threw his arms around his daughter.

"Willow said you were headed for the factory," he blurted. "What on the round blue Earth were you thinking? This whole place looks like it was hit by a tornado. There are fire trucks everywhere. What did you do? Are you all right?" He checked her over for scrapes and bruises, finding many. He hugged her close.

"I'm OK, Dad." Lucy held him tightly.

The sheriff entered the room on Silas's heels, the spurs on her cowboy boots jingling. "Where's Fisher?" she demanded, a hand on the gun at her hip. "The fire department is having a heck of a time upstairs. Looks like there was some kind of explosion."

"Yes, an explosion," Fisher hastily agreed. "There was a gas leak. Thank goodness you're here."

"Who are all these people?" The sheriff paled as she recognised the English teacher. "Stricks? Millepoids. Chelon! Holy smokes, they're all here," she shouted. "Somebody get a medic!"

"Please, we just want to go home," said Mrs Stricks. "There's no need for more doctors."

"How did you get down here?" asked Sheriff Pryce, flabbergasted. "Some of these people have been missing for weeks, for Pete's sake."

"We had an allergic reaction to the new sweetener," Mr Millepoids calmly explained. "We needed specialised medical attention, which we have received." He wiped a streak of yellow paint from his forehead with the back of his now normal, human hand.

An allergic reaction? Lucy's mouth fell open. *Are you flippin' kidding me?*

"With Mr Fisher's generous assistance," said Mrs Stricks, "the issue has now been resolved. Isn't that right, Richard?"

Mr Fisher nodded curtly.

Lucy watched in dismay as each of the adults lied to the sheriff with a straight face. She had never seen such coordination outside of an anthill. *Nobody in here is telling the truth. Why?* And then something occurred to her that made her feel like a twig swaying at the top of a giant sequoia. *Is Mr Fisher RIGHT? Is there something wrong with the people in Sticky Pines?*

"Yes. An allergic reaction." Fisher coughed. "It involves proprietary information. All very hush-hush. Shareholders," he added.

"I cannot fathom," the sheriff seethed, "why no one notified me about this sooner. What does any of this have to do with that fire-alarm mayhem upstairs?" Her eyes landed on Lucy, huddled in her father's arms. "Sladan." Sheriff Pryce rubbed her temples with her fingers. "Of course you're here. I'm surprised you didn't call this gorram nonsense in yourself."

Everyone focused on Lucy.

The sheriff bent down. "All right, kid," she said. "Now's your chance. If there's anything you want to tell me, say it now. I don't care if it's Bigfoot, mermaids or poltergeists. What did you see, girl?"

Lucy had been waiting to hear those words her entire life. She looked around at the many faces in the room. Millepoids, shifting uncomfortably in his green gown. Her concerned and clueless father, unaware that his job was very much in jeopardy, along with everyone else's in town. Mrs Stricks, silently imploring Lucy not to say anything. And then there was Milo, who had gone against his own father to defend her quest for the Truth. But if she told the truth, what would she be exposing? And at what cost?

She had always wanted to be the first person to prove to the world that there's a vast inexplicable universe outside our puny understanding of reality – but at the expense of her teacher, her neighbours, her family? She felt like she was going to throw up.

"Go ahead," said Milo. "Tell them."

"Um…" said Lucy.

"Go on," said Silas.

Milo squeezed her hand. "I've got your back."

Which only made what she was about to do even harder. "It sounds crazy but…" She shut her eyes tightly and gritted her teeth. "It's like they said. Milo and I left the carnival and we got lost in the woods. Somehow we ended up at the factory." Each word felt like a knife to her soul. "Everything was on fire. There was an explosion and we ran down here for help. Then we just … stumbled on the missing people." She slumped under the weight of her weary shoulders. "I'm just happy everyone's OK." She half-heartedly raised a fist in the air.

When she opened her eyes, Milo was staring at her as though she had just run over his new puppy.

"So much for the Truth." He stormed off, hitting her with his elbow on the way out.

Lucy touched her arm. Of all the many

injuries she had sustained that day, this one stung the most.

Mr Fisher smiled triumphantly. "You see?" he said. "Just as I explained. Let's discuss the rest of this matter in private." He patted the sheriff on the shoulder.

"We certainly will," Sheriff Pryce replied. "Nobody leaves until they talk to a police officer," she announced to the crowd. "Snakes alive, this is going to be a lot of paperwork." She spat on the floor and ushered the formerly missing Sticky Pines residents into the hallway with the others.

"Sir." Silas extended his hand to Mr Fisher. "I just want to thank you for helping my girl."

Mr Fisher shook his hand. "Of course," he said, graciously insincere. "I'm so glad neither of our children was seriously injured."

Lucy felt like her head was going to implode.

Silas wiped a happy tear on his sleeve. "Luce." He guided his daughter towards his boss.

"Thank Mr Fisher for everything he did for you today."

Lucy stood before the man, stone-faced. "Thanks."

"Any time," said Fisher.

CHAPTER 19

Owl Be Back

Sticky Pines had gone relatively quiet in the two weeks since the harrowing events at the Nu Co. factory. Autumn had settled in with a cloak of crispy brown leaves and endless cloudy skies. There were no more unusual creature sightings, no disappearances. Everything was, on the surface, mind-meltingly ordinary.

Mrs Stricks returned to school the week after she was found. She threw a pizza party for her students, and provided a vague explanation involving an unexpected stay at the hospital. People raised few questions, and those that went unanswered stayed that way.

Most of the townspeople remembered Fisher's carnival quite fondly. Local news reporters, including the de-fanged Carlos Felina, declared that they were looking forward to the Nu Co. Par-T in Da Pines next year and for many more to come. Everyone involved in the monstrous events seemed happy to let it all evaporate into the mist of rumour that often hung over the last and least-known corner of the New World. Everyone, of course, but Lucy Sladan and Milo Fisher.

It was a Saturday morning in early October, and everyone in the Sladan household was recovering from eating cookies for breakfast. Each family member had made their own batch. Willow's Millepoids-inspired banana nut chocolate chips had been the overwhelming favourite, handily beating Lucy's rather uninspired snickerdoodles. As a reward, Silas had taken Willow owl pellet hunting for the day.

Lucy sat at her desk staring wistfully out the window at a pair of ravens squawking on a skeletal birch, silhouetted against the silver sky. Her room was unrecognisably tidy, her desk free of anything but a lamp and a laptop, her figurines dusted and arranged according to size rather than genre. The "Keep Out, Unbelievers" sign on the door had been replaced with one that read simply: "Please Knock".

For the past two weeks, Lucy had been trying to relax, to not ask questions, to stop thinking about lies and Nucralose and monsters and everything that had happened since the Fishers came to town. To stop thinking about Milo Fisher full stop. It wasn't working.

Errol rose from the beanbag chair and trotted to the attic doorway to greet Miranda.

Lucy's mother regarded the too-tidy surroundings with concern. She scratched Errol behind the ears. "Are you planning on staying up here all weekend?"

"What else is there to do?" said Lucy.

Miranda smoothed the covers on the not-so-skilfully made bed. "Why don't you take

Errol for a walk?"

Upon hearing the "W" word, the dog jumped up from the floor, tail wagging and tongue hanging out the side of his mouth.

"Mph." Lucy threw up her arms limply. "What's the point?"

"The point is that the doggy," Miranda said in a voice designed to make Errol bounce from one massive foot to the other, "clearly wants to go outside."

Errol barked affirmatively.

"And the rest of us are tired of watching you sulk," she added.

Errol barked again.

"But there's nothing out there," said Lucy. "Not for me, anyways." She lolled in her chair. "And even if there is, nobody will ever know about it."

"If a tree falls in the forest and no one is around to hear it," said Miranda, "does that mean you have to live the rest of your life as a couch potato?"

Errol whimpered.

"Fine, I'll go outside," said Lucy. She laboriously clambered out of her chair, the dog grinning from ear to ear. "But it's because Errol's all excited, not because existence has any meaning."

"Whatever you say, spud." Miranda walked over to the attic landing. "Take a snack, take your time," she said. "And don't worry about me, all alone in this empty house with nothing but a good book and a bubble bath." She traipsed down the stairs, humming.

Lucy laced up her boots and threw on her red hoodie. She stopped by the kitchen, where her mom was tidying up the dishes, and grabbed a bag of leftover cookies to take with her.

"Later, tater!" Miranda called through the kitchen window as Lucy ran out of the garage with Errol at her heels.

Lucy inhaled the late-morning air, savouring the scent of forced freedom. She saluted Arnold the crooked tree as they entered the woods. The larches were putting on a glorious golden show before their needles fell to the winds of winter. The deep greens and blues of the other pines would soon be the only colour in the landscape.

Lucy practised her balancing skills on a rotting log while Errol did his business behind a bulbous cedar.

Her head jerked around hopefully at a rustling sound in the bushes. *Fish?*

She hadn't seen Milo since the factory. At first, she thought he'd been sent off to boarding school, like he'd said back at the carnival. However, her mother informed her that he was still showing up to class, though his attendance had become "erratic".

Lucy couldn't imagine what must be going on inside the Fisher household. She felt guilty and angry, often both at the same time. The look on Milo's face when she had lied still haunted her.

Errol barked excitedly and dived into the bushes, chasing a dodging and darting rabbit out on to the path. *Of course Milo's not following me. He hates me.*

If Lucy had stopped kicking herself and looked skyward, she might have noticed that something was indeed following her: hovering near the treetops was a set of four blue lights glowing dimly in the daylight, set in a diamond formation, buzzing softly.

She soon found herself someplace she had headed to almost instinctively: the Strickses' cabin. The carved owl statues were back on their perches on the porch steps. They had been freshly repainted, but the owl in flight seemed to have permanently lost a wing. Lucy couldn't remember if she, Milo, the search party or the monster formerly known as the Other Mrs Stricks had knocked it over. It all seemed so very long ago.

"What do you want?" said a gruff voice. The Other Mrs Stricks was standing behind the screen door. It was the first time Lucy had seen her since the day she had turned into a Bigwoof.

She was pleased to see the old woman in her usual good spirits.

"I've been meaning to stop by to say thank you," said Lucy. "For, you know, saving us from the bear and everything."

"You should tell your friend not to mess with cubs," said the Other Mrs Stricks. "Mama bears don't like it."

"Yeah, well," Lucy kicked a dirt clod, "he's not really my friend any more."

"I'm sorry to hear that. Twyla says he's a good kid, all things considered."

"May I come in?" asked Lucy. "I brought cookies." She pulled the bag out of her front pocket.

"Did someone say cookies?" Lucy heard Mrs Stricks call from inside the cabin.

The Other Mrs Stricks glowered at the overcast sky. "All right, Sladan, come in. But make it quick." She opened the tattered screen door with a creak. "We've got somewhere to be."

Lucy signalled for Errol to wait outside. He

lay down and rolled in a pile of leaves as she ascended the porch steps.

The cosy cabin had been cleaned up, though it was not entirely restored from its previous destruction. A new cuckoo clock adorned the wall in place of the one that had been smashed to smithereens. The broken shelves had been swept away, the salvaged knick-knacks lined up meticulously on the dining-room table.

Lucy shook a small snow globe featuring Mount St Helens. The glittery fake snow flurried around the peak and slowly settled once more at the bottom of the tiny tableau.

Four wooden crates were arranged at the centre of the room in place of the shattered coffee table. Sitting behind them in a wooden folding chair was Mrs Stricks, wearing her customary shorts and a bedazzled floral sweatshirt.

Lucy plunked the bag of cookies on a crate and offered one to each of the ladies.

Mrs Stricks took a bite of one of Silas's oatmeal cookies. "Pardon our dust," she said.

"This place looks way better than last time I saw it," said Lucy.

"Turning into a big hairy monster is messy business," said the Other Mrs Stricks, crumbs spittling on to her rainbow shawl.

"Would you like some tea?" said Mrs Stricks.

"No thank you," said Lucy. The events of the weeks prior swirled unendingly through her mind. "Do you feel back to normal?" she asked. "After everything, I mean…"

"As normal as one ever feels." The Other Mrs Stricks wrapped her scarf tightly around her broad shoulders. "It takes more than a little forced transfiguration to scare me."

"Don't be ridiculous, Esther," Mrs Stricks admonished. "It was all quite upsetting. None of us have ever experienced anything like that before. I hope to never again."

"The lack of self-control was unsatisfactory," the Other Mrs Stricks frowned, flexing her fingers.

Lucy offered her another cookie. "I have a few

questions I'd like to ask, if that's OK."

"Questions, questions," tsked the Other Mrs Stricks. "Can't you just leave well enough alone, girl? You saved the day, didn't you? What more do you want?" She took the cookie.

"I want to know the truth," said Lucy. "The whole truth."

Mrs Stricks clasped her hands and furrowed her brow sympathetically. "Sometimes the truth isn't so simple. Sometimes people keep secrets for a reason."

"But ... I *lied*," said Lucy. "I lied because you asked me to." She tried to suppress the anger welling up inside her. "And ever since then I've felt ... I've lost..." She couldn't find the words. "Please, you have to help me understand."

"All you need to know," said the Other Mrs Stricks, waving her cookie matter-of-factly, "is when to stop asking questions."

The cuckoo clock came to life to announce the hour. A small red bird emerged from a green door. It cocked its head from side to side and chirped twelve times, its eyes lit up in electric blue.

Mrs Stricks stood. "I'm afraid it's time to go," she said. "We have an appointment."

"Wait." Lucy gripped her teacher's sleeve. "Please. Not everything makes sense to me."

"That sounds uncomfortable," said the Other Mrs Stricks, "but it's not our problem." She dusted crumbs from her green muumuu and fished out one of Miranda's powdery polvoróns for the road.

"Look, Lucy—" Mrs Stricks began.

"Why didn't you tell everyone what happened?" Lucy interrupted. "Why didn't you tell the truth?"

Mrs Stricks shook her head. "My poor dear. I know how difficult this must be for you."

"You can't always get what you want," said the Other Mrs Stricks. "Don't they teach the Rolling Stones in school?"

"It's all for the greater good, dear, please believe me," said Mrs Stricks. "Someday, perhaps, you'll understand. For now, it's best that you forget any of this ever happened."

"Are you serious?" Lucy screwed up her face in disbelief. "I'm sorry, but that's bunk."

"This is like trying to teach a banana slug to go fly fishing," grunted the Other Mrs Stricks.

"Mr Fisher is not going to forget what happened," said Lucy.

"Oh please." The Other Mrs Stricks snorted. "After what we've been through over the years, I'm hardly afraid of a middle-aged man in a tie."

"A middle-aged man in a tie is a powerful thing to be these days, Esther," muttered Mrs Stricks. "Perhaps we shouldn't underestimate him."

"You shouldn't," said Lucy. "The guy's nuts, believe me." She scooted to the edge of her seat. "Fisher was making crazy claims about the people of Sticky Pines. He thinks you're *dangerous*, you and everyone who changed. He wants to *dissect* you, and maybe me too. If we all just went on the news and told our story, I've got plenty of proof that could—"

"I told you, Lucita," Mrs Stricks cut her off. "We're not talking to the press."

"But why not?" Lucy demanded. "What was Mr Fisher talking about? Is there really something weird about Sticky Pines?"

"You've got our answer," said the Other Mrs Stricks. "What more do you require from us?"

"Require?" said Lucy. She pounded the milk crate with a fist. "I require that people start telling the truth for once," she declared. "I require that the world not run on lies."

"That's not our fault," the Other Mrs Stricks objected. "Talk to your congressman."

Mrs Stricks gave her wife a grave look. "She's right about one thing, Esther. We *have* been noticed. We knew it was coming sooner or later, it always does. Human technology has advanced by leaps and bounds in the blink of an eye. Maybe we need to face facts…"

The Other Mrs Stricks drained her teacup and slammed it on the crate with a hollow thud.

"We've been through this, Twyla. Now is not the time to bring in outsiders."

"I'm not an outsider," said Lucy. "I'm from Sticky Pines, for cripe's sake. I'm on your side. Especially if Fisher's on the other side. All these questions are eating me alive. Please," she begged. "Someone just tell me what's going on!"

The cuckoo emerged once more, eyes glowing red this time to match its plumage. Its wooden head flicked from side to side. A rumble of thunder punctuated its insistent squawks.

"Your clock's broken," said Lucy.

"That's the alarm," said Mrs Stricks.

"Since when do cuckoo clocks have alarms?" asked Lucy.

"Since when are telephones maps and magazines?" the Other Mrs Stricks retorted. She stood and stretched, twisting her upper body, her joints popping satisfactorily. "Oh, maybe you're right, Twyla. The girl has proven she can keep a secret, hasn't she?"

Mrs Stricks's eyes grew wide. "Are you saying

what I think you're saying?"

"What's she saying?" asked Lucy.

Another clap of thunder struck, this time closer.

"Come, Twyla." The Other Mrs Stricks fanned out her rainbow shawl like the wings of a macaw. "It's time to go."

"Esther," said Mrs Stricks, alarmed. "Maybe we should wait." She glanced anxiously at Lucy. "She's not ready."

"Oh, the girl's on to us," said the Other Mrs Stricks. "Look at her. She won't let up now. Not after all she's seen."

"She's only a child," said Mrs Stricks, lowering her voice.

"I'm practically a teenager," Lucy interjected.

"Precisely," said the Other Mrs Stricks. "She's a child. If she talks, nobody will believe her. What better way to test the consequences of new knowledge on the dominant species?"

The dominant ... what?

"We have all agreed that now is not the time

to take such risks," hissed Mrs Stricks. "The humans are larval."

Larval?

"And highly volatile, I know." The Other Mrs Stricks stroked Mrs Stricks's forearm. "But their abilities have caught up to us. They're on the precipice of a new phase of existence, whether they, or we, are ready."

Lucy raised her hand. "Um. What?"

"Oh for goodness' sake, Esther," wailed Mrs Stricks. "I hope you know what you're doing."

"What *are* you doing?" The conversation seemed to have left Lucy behind entirely.

"Sometimes," the Other Mrs Stricks smiled sweetly at her wife, "all we can do is act and hope for the best."

With that, she tossed her shawl into the air, the hand-knit cloth billowing around her. There was an odd piney scent that seemed to emanate from her body. Her skin swelled, shuddered and jellified. The cloth hit the floor as colourless goopy slime dripped down her body like sap on a sticky pine.

Lucy yelped and leapt behind a stack of folding chairs. The Other Mrs Stricks continued to sweat slime until her entire body was as transparent as water, as though she were made of the ooze herself. Suddenly, her shape lost form and she splashed to the floor in a thick puddle.

Lucy gaped in shock as the woman vanished. Atop the crumpled rainbow shawl sat a barred owl with a grey-ringed face. The same owl that had followed Milo and Lucy through the woods on the day of the carnival. It cocked its head mischievously at Lucy and kicked the shawl with its taloned toes. It hooted at Mrs Stricks, who was wringing her hands anxiously across the room. The bird flapped its powerful, silent wings and took off through the open window.

Lucy ran over and gawped as the owl soared higher and higher, the storm swirling overhead. Before the Other Mrs Stricks could reach the clouds, a bolt of lightning shot down from the heavens. BXOWM! It struck her, and she disappeared in a burst of feathery empyreal radiance. Errol ran in circles below, barking at the sky.

Lucy fell back to the floor. She pulled the rainbow shawl towards her, leaving a trail of rapidly evaporating goop in its wake. She looked up at her teacher.

"Th-the Other Mrs Stricks," Lucy stammered. "What is— How did she…?"

"I'm so sorry to spring all this on you, my dear," said Mrs Stricks. She chewed her bottom lip. "But you did ask…"

"Mrs Stricks," said Lucy, every cell in her body tingling with wonder, "what are you?"

The teacher shrugged apologetically. "I must be off. You can show yourself out, can't you, Lucy dear? I trust you'll keep all this between us." With that, she liquefied into an owl, smaller than the first, and flew out the window.

Outside the cabin, Errol watched the horizon as

a second bird disappeared in a bolt of lightning. Then he noticed something even weirder. It was that buzzy flying machine, the one that had been zooming around the forest for weeks. It was hovering over the cabin, level with the chimney. Errol growled, baring his teeth menacingly. The machine darted downward, and the dog yelped and low-tailed it under the porch. The unidentified flying object was close enough now that any human observer might recognise it for what it was: a high-tech drone, controlled remotely from afar. Attached to its base were four blue lights and a small video camera.

Not so very far away, in a dungeon-like tunnel made of spiralled stones, a man in a tie sat at a desk in front of a computer.

Behind Mr Fisher, Doctor Quittan was busy writing various combinations of abnormal DNA sequences on a large whiteboard.

Doctor Vink sauntered into the Nu Co. surveillance office. "The factory rebuild is continuing apace," he said. "Unfortunately, the FDA says we'll have to run more tests before we can sell Nucralose to the general public."

Mr Fisher pointed at his laptop screen. "What do you make of this?"

Doctor Vink watched the events recorded by the drone. "Did I just watch a couple of birds get electrocuted?" He chuckled. "Planning on releasing a viral video, are we?"

"That is not natural animal behaviour," said Doctor Quittan. "You should consider getting a zoologist down here in addition to the chemical engineers."

"And an arboriculturist," Doctor Vink nodded. "I still can't make head or tail of the trees."

"I think we're going to need more than that." Fisher directed the drone over the roof of the log cabin as a girl with purple hair ran outside, jumping and waving her arms at the spot where the owls had disappeared.

"What are you going to do about the Sladan

girl?" asked Quittan, adding letters to a genetic sequence on the whiteboard. "The brat keeps getting in the way."

"She's just a child," said Vink.

"Is she?" asked Fisher. He watched as Lucy turned and spotted the drone. She jumped in alarm, squinted at the video camera attached to its base and yelled something Fisher couldn't hear. He flew the drone closer, hovering it tauntingly, a couple of metres over her head.

"Either way," said Fisher, a smirk creeping across his face, "she knows we're watching."

Lucy picked up a shoe-sized rock from the Strickses' dirt driveway, took aim and chucked it at the drone. The picture on Fisher's screen vanished, his smile along with it.

ACKNOWLEDGEMENTS

Writing this book has been quite a journey, and I've met many fellow travellers along the way. I offer my deepest thanks to the following: my wonderful editor Kirsty Stansfield and agent Laura West, for believing in this story and delving deep into the world of Sticky Pines; the intrepid team at Nosy Crow who worked so brilliantly to make this series fly; my first reader and first fan, Anna Tullis, who cares about Lucy and Milo as much as I do; Sara Grant and Linda Buckley-Archer, for their wise instruction and enthusiastic hammering of my prose; readers, friends and family members Adam, Paula, Clare, Katie, Asya, Marek, Reeve, Shami, Gwynne and Sadie for being an honest and encouraging early audience; Ash, the first kid to explore Sticky Pines, whose excited response gave me the confidence to keep going; Lara Downie, for her beautiful photography and general awesomeness; the Swaggers, for making sense of the mad world of publishing in the most amusing way possible; my mother and brother, for their love and support through the delightfully thick and impossibly thin; Monkey, the most adorable and entertaining companion a human could ask for; and JGR, for too many joys to share – thank you for being there, in all your exacting glory. Finally, thanks to all the imaginary worlds I've visited, which have been indispensable to my reality.